WITHDRAWN
From School of Visual Arts
Library Collection

# The Failure To Rescue

**Other books by Herbert Druks**

**Harry S Truman and the Russians, 1945 - 1953
From Truman Through Johnson (Two volumes)
The City in Western Civilization, Volume I**

# The Failure To Rescue

By

Herbert Druks, Ph.D.

Professor of Judaic Studies & History
Brooklyn College

Robert Speller & Sons, Publishers, Inc.
New York, New York 10010

©1977 by Herbert Druks
ISBN 0-8315-0175-8
FIRST EDITION
Printed in the United States of America

## CONTENTS

Introduction ................................................... vii
The Doors Were Closed ..........................................1
Seas of Indifference ............................................17
Speak Not for the Jews Are Burning ......................29
Failures To Rescue ............................................57
The 982 ........................................................79
To the Promised Land .......................................83
Bibliography ..................................................102
Index ..........................................................107

# INTRODUCTION

Many people have suffered greatly, but few suffered as much as the Jewish people of Europe, Russia and the Middle East. From 1933 to 1945, nearly one third of its number was exterminated by European Nazidom and its collaborators. A good portion of the six million could have been saved if only refuge had been established. But it did not happen that way.

Most of the world's statesmen and international politicians did not care as to what would happen to the Jews, and Jewish leadership in the "free world" of Britain and America proved unwilling or unable to act with decisiveness and eclat on behalf of European Jewry. The Jewish leadership was too badly divided and frightened of anti-Semitism to do anything. And there were even some American Jews who did not want their fellow Jews to come to America because they were afraid that their own position might in some way be hampered, perhaps, by the growth of anti-Semitisim.

Hitler and his followers saw that no one wanted the Jews, no one cared, and so he continued to use them as his scapegoat. Some have maintained that nothing would have stopped Hitler from killing the Jews, that he did not listen to public protests.

But I wonder. When German and world public opinion challenged the Nazi policy of mercy killing, it was discontinued. Even the evil and crazed killers of Germany led by Adolf Hitler seemed to have responded to public opinion. But instead of protests there was deliberate suppression of information about the Nazi atrocities against the Jews. There was suppression by British and American governmental leaders as well as by some Jewish leaders in America.

Instead of keeping Palestine - Erez Israel - open so that Jews could continue to go there, Britain closed that avenue of refuge in order to pacify Arab extremists, and President Roosevelt supported Great Britain.

Instead of bombing the railroad lines that led to the concentration camps and crematoriums, British and American officials claimed that they could not afford the planes even though those planes passed the camps on regular missions. The German Nazis and their European collaborators could not have killed so many Jews so quickly without the railroad system, the gas chambers and the crematoriums. The inmates of the camps and the ghettos might have gained greater hope for resistance if they had seen that the Allies cared enough to bomb Nazi death factories. But no such bombing took place. And when the Jews of Warsaw and other cities and camps revolted against the Nazis, there was no help forthcoming from the Allies.

After studying, researching and teaching this history for the past 15 years, I feel it my duty to present this book which I have researched in American Government Archives, Zionist Archives, the World Jewish Congress Archives and various manuscript collections. I do this especially for my students so that they may learn more fully of how the so-called "free world" - the "good guys" of Western Civilization and the many American-Jewish organizations failed to help save the Jews of Europe.

And I present this study so that the less powerful states of this world might learn to become less dependent on the goodwill of such powerful states as the U.S. and the U.S.S.R. Israeli leaders, in particular, might learn from this history that they can no more depend on the goodwill and word of Nixon or Kissinger than of F.D.R. They might learn that unless they can fend for themselves, they may not survive.

If all the heavens were parchment and the oceans ink and all mankind were scribes not in a thousand years could the story of the crimes committed against the Jewish people during the Holocaust be told. It is my hope that this book will add some additional light to that history, and that it will encourage others to likewise seriously and honestly study it.

I would like to acknowledge my thanks to the National Archives, the Zionist Archives of New York, the Department of State, the F.D.R. Library, Brandeis University Manuscript Division, the Library of Congress, the Joint Distribution Committee, the American Jewish Committee, and the World Jewish Congress for permitting me to use the papers and records of: Justice Louis D. Brandeis, Judge Julian W. Mack, Benjamin V. Cohen, J.D.C., American Jewish Committee, Robert Szold, Franklin D. Roosevelt, Stephen S. Wise, American Zionist Emergency Council, World Zionist Organization, Jewish Agency, Bernard Baruch, Breckinridge Long, William E. Dodd, Lawrence Steinhardt, Admiral William Leahy, Charles Ross and Samuel Rosenman.

I would also like to thank the following people for granting me interviews. Benjamin Akzin, Benjamin V. Cohen, Ira Hirschmann, Herbert Katzki, Maurice Perlzweig, Emanuel Neumann, Gerhard Riegner, and Samuel Rosenman.

# The Failure To Rescue

# CHAPTER I

# The Doors Were Closed

Nazi Germany and its allies started World War II. Nazi Germany and its allies murdered six million Jews. There need be little debate concerning those facts, but one must add that it would not have been possible for Nazi Germany to start that war if the 1918 victors had not foresaken their responsibilities and permitted acts of aggression to go unpunished from 1931 through 1938. Nor would it have been possible for Nazi Germany to destroy six million Jews if the free world had not chosen to shut its doors to the Jews. What did the U.S., the most powerful free nation in the world at that time, do to help save human beings from extermination? Did America open its gates to the persecuted and homeless? Did the Roosevelt Administration concern itself with the rescue of Jewry from annihilation?

During the holocaust years, President Roosevelt occasionally expressed the hope that America would again become a place of refuge, but such expressions of sympathy were only temporary and meant little, for the Jews were not even admitted under existing quotas and no effort was made to change the quota laws. America failed to provide even a temporary asylum and only sought to shirk its responsibility by asking other nations to help. Only in the last moments of the war did the Roosevelt Administration admit a few hundred Jews to a temporary "Free Port" in Fort Ontario, Oswego, New York, as an example for others to follow, but nobody followed.

As European Jewry sought asylum, most European states maintained that they were already overpopulated, and they asked that an international organization relocate them to the Americas. Europe chose to ignore the fact that the Jews were Europeans and the "New World" nations claimed that their economic dislocation and unemployment prohibited them from helping the refugees.

# 2    The Doors Were Closed

When the British were asked to make Palestine available to the Jews they claimed, even in 1933, that the area could not accommodate Jews.(1)

By 1933, there seemed to be no place for the persecuted. Some would sigh that it was a shame to see people so mistreated, but few would even sigh, and fewer still would welcome them. No one wanted the Jews.

Britain was perhaps the most callous of free states. From 1933 through May, 1948, Britain did all it could to keep the Jews not only out of Palestine, but out of every other possible place including a projected U.S. of Africa. It was as if there was a tacit conspiracy with the Nazis to destroy the Jews.

In 1935, the United States refused to participate in the League's efforts to help the refugees.(2) The established policy was that people would be admitted only on an individual basis, that it would not be "appropriate for the President to support an appeal for assistance for one particular class of refugees" or as President Roosevelt himself put it to a constituent, the mass exodus of Jews from Germany would not "affect this country much for everything would be on a quota basis."(3) America was to be made safe from the persecuted.

Top government officials seemed to have no idea of the danger to which the Jews were exposed. Perhaps they just pretended ignorance? On March 26, 1933, Secretary of State Cordell Hull told Rabbi Stephen S. Wise, President of the American Jewish Congress, and Cyrus Adler, President of the Jewish Theological Seminary of America, that the persecutions in Germany would soon come to an end. He felt hopeful that in view of the reported attitude of high German officials and the "evidence of amelioration already indicated, that the situation, which has caused such widespread concern...will soon revert to normal."(4)

In his testimony before the Anglo-American Committee of Inquiry on January 8, 1946, Zionist leader Emanuel Neumann recalled the danger which Jewry faced during the war period and the callous indifference of the free world:

> Now and then, here and there, something was done to alleviate suffering and to find refuge....But...all in all, and viewed in relation to the staggering proportions of the problem...practical achievement was virtually nill.
>
> We have reached the point now, at which the admission of

900...refugees to this country - and I'm proud of my country, but this is a fact - as a special emergency measure a year and a half ago was hailed as a great humanitarian act. They were not permitted to settle anywhere in the U.S., but were kept in a camp at Oswego for 18 months. Only a fortnight ago they were finally permitted to apply for permanent residence. Oswego epitomizes the situation.

**Evian Conference**

In March 1938, Germany annexed Austria and life for Austria's Jews ceased. F.D.R. wondered aloud if more could be done to help. He recalled how America had been a place of refuge for so many in the past. "Why couldn't we offer them again a place of refuge at this time?"(5) The sentiment was there, but the action wasn't. The President refused to have the immigration laws changed and sought to solve the problem by initiating a world conference on refugees. This conference was held at Evian, France in July 1938.

Roosevelt's plan was to have the participating states, supported by private funds, provide asylum to the refugees according to existing immigration restrictions and quotas. He invited such leading American figures as James G. MacDonald, Samuel Cavert, Louis Kennedy, Henry Morgenthau Jr., Bernard Baruch and Rabbi Stephen S. Wise to a White House conference called to find funds for future settlement projects. It was then that a President's Advisory Committee on Political Refugees was organized to help the Jewish refugees, but the word Jew was omitted from the title of the Committee.

When the newly established Committee convened in May 1938, to discuss the forthcoming Evian Conference, Administration officials rejected Rabbi Wise's suggestion that Britain be urged to liberalize its Palestine policy. They insisted that the Palestine question "would stir up bitter passions and might even lead to disruption of the entire conference."(6) The President's Committee was advised that the states participating at Evian were not anxious to admit Jews, that they had accepted invitations only "because they did not wish to appear before international opinion as completely standing aside," and that the U.S. was no better since its quotas were such that "little possible action" could be expected.(7) Since Palestine was excluded as a possible place of refuge and the attending states were unwilling to admit immigrants, the conference was a joke. But the persecuted did not laugh.

At the Evian Conference many expressed their sympathy for the plight of the refugees but few supported their words with deeds. The European states feared a new surge of refugees in their midst, and American states such as Venezuela, Uruguay and Chile found that they could not be hospitable, and even refused to engage in any debate critical of Germany. With the exception of the Dominican Republic's offer to accommodate 100,000(8) homeless, no nation made any substantial offer. Born in discussion, thriving in discussion, the conference ended by creating a debating society called the Intergovernmental Committee on Political Refugees. Again, the word Jew was not to be found in their vocabulary. The Intergovernmental Committee, ordained to organize orderly immigration from Germany with the help of the German Government, and to secure places of refuge, was a screen behind which the so-called "civilized" states hid. It was a dead end agency. Hitler blatantly spoke of letting Jews out of Germany "even on luxury ships" but no one wanted to receive them. Late in 1938, United States representatives in Germany reported that German officials wanted to see an end to the persecutions of the Jews in order to put an end to the international hatred which such measures created against Germany. Goering envisioned the complete elimination from Germany of all Jews within three years and he was prepared to enter into bilateral arrangements on the refugee question. While Americans observed a deep-seated anti-Semitism in Germany, they reported that some Germans were outspoken in their resentment of German brinkmanship and anti-Jewish excesses. Some Germans seemed to feel that those excesses would defeat the desired aim of a reasonable Jewish emigration from Germany.(9) But by October 1938, some Jewish leaders in America, like Emanuel Neumann, were saying:

> As for European Jewry - it's finished so far as the Continent at least is concerned. Even France is no longer sound. Middle class people in the railway trains in France repeat the propaganda emanating from Goebbels. One lady told me all in one breath: Churchill and Eden were "des Bolshevists;" the Jews were "des internationaux;" the Jews were making trouble in Palestine...Mussolini and Chamberlain were the great statesmen of the world and France would be alright if it had a different

kind of government...." The situation in Central and Eastern Europe is appalling. Here the Jews are virtually leaderless. Again in the case of Vienna...I don't understand why the big Jewish organizations of New York, London and Paris leave the situation to drift from bad to worse without sending their representatives immediately into the distressed areas, not so much to dole out money as to guide, take counsel, give direction and leadership.

But it's *America,* America alone that can save us. We must have a new birth of Zionism in America which will grip all - from the infant in the cradle...The fearful cataclysm in Europe must be dramatized and driven home to them as never before and every man must be terrorized if need be into doing his bit. The five million Jews of America can and must do the trick politically and financially.(10)

A year after its formation, the Intergovernmental Committee reported that some progress had been made in negotiations with the Dominican Republic, British Guiana and the Philippines for the settlement of the refugees. But that's all it had to report. In view of the ineffectiveness of the Intergovernmental Committee, some officials like Robert Pell, Assistant Secretary of State for European Affairs, urged that it be scrapped, and wondered if America was sincerely interested in finding a solution to the refugee problem or if it was just using the refugee question to promote policies hostile to Germany. Meetings were held, hopes raised, but the refugees were not helped. He found diplomatic conferences on refugees a waste of time and a terrible "source of disillusionment" for the refugees. More could be done, argued Pell, if America were to help existing projects. President Roosevelt found Pell's arguments unacceptable. The President did not go along with "limited projects" but favored a "solution of the refugee problem in the broadest sense...." because the world would be faced with ten to twenty million displaced persons after the war. Even if the Intergovernmental Committee made "pretty speeches" he believed it was worth keeping "very definitely alive."(11)

Administrative officials like Undersecretary of State Sumner Welles and Secretary of Labor Frances Perkins advised the President to ease immigration restrictions and use any possible means to help the refugees, but Roosevelt insisted that little could be done unless Congress were given practical plans supported by other nations. The public seemed opposed to any changes that would admit more refugees and Roosevelt refused to tangle with such public sentiment. Fortune Poll of April 1938, indicated that 67.4% were opposed to changes, and in 1939, the same poll indicated that 83% were opposed to changes in the quotas.(12)

**Crystal Night**

When a young Polish Jew, distraught by the German abuse of fellow Jews, killed a German diplomat in France, it gave the German Government and the Nazis a convenient excuse for mass attacks and executions of Jews on November 10, 1938. The pogroms began in the early morning hours and did not end until Jewish property was pilfered, synagogues destroyed, some forty Jews beaten to death and 20,000 arrested. And then the German Government imposed a fine on the Jewish people of Germany, claiming that they had provoked the attacks.

Four days later, Rabbi Stephen S. Wise noted that the Council of Jewish Organizations had urged Jewish groups to refrain from public protests because they feared that such protests would only serve to stimulate further attacks on Germany's Jews. (13)

And when Lord Rothschild of England would come to America in February of 1939, with vivid reports of the concentration camps, some Department of State officials claimed that he was a propagandist:

> Lord Rothschild gave a vivid description of conditions in concentration camps, which he stated was based on first hand accounts of persons who had escaped to England. His view of the whole situation was exceedingly pessimistic, so pessimistic that I cannot but believe he is indulging in propaganda. As an example he expressed the belief that all Jews in Germany would be dead within two years.(14)

Siding with such State Department officials was Samuel I. Rosenman, one of the President's advisors and a Jew. He maintained that it was not "desirable or practical to recommend any change in the quota provisions of our immigration laws."(15)

Newton Jenkins, a candidate for the Democratic nomination for the U.S. Senate seat from Illinois telegraphed Cordell Hull and protested vigorously against the admission of "racial refugees from Austria and elsewhere." He claimed that there were "far too many of these racial elements" and those already here had gained far more than their just share of power over U.S. finance, industry, radio, the press, government and the State Department. And he urged that America take away from these elements what they had seized and return it to the American people as Hitler did in Germany.(16)

President Roosevelt had little desire to defy Congress or public sentiment, and the American immigration laws were to be only more rigorously enforced despite the continuous persecutions and slaughter of European Jewry.

That innocent people were terrorized in response to orders handed down by the German Government was no secret to Roosevelt. As Assistant Secretary of State George Messersmith saw it, Germany's terror policies against part of its people and threats against the "rest of the world with further action if it should even pass censure, is an irresponsible act that our government cannot pass unnoticed."(17) On November 15, 1938, F.D.R. issued the following proclamation:

> The news of the past few days from Germany has deeply shocked public opinion in the U.S. Such news from any part of the world would inevitably produce a similar profound reaction among American people in every part of the nation.
> I myself could scarcely believe that such things could occur in a 20th Century Civilization.

The American President seemed shocked. The "free world," so-called, seemed shocked. Ambassadors were recalled from Germany, but Jews were still not given refuge. The President felt compelled to ask his State Department to furnish "any information you have in regard to possible places for Jewish colonization in any part of the world." The President thought that if America, because of its immigration laws, fears and economic dislocation could not admit the refugees, then other countries should be found that would admit them.(18) America did not receive them, nor were other places found for them.

Some American Jewish leaders like Cyrus Adler, President of the Jewish Theological Seminary of America, seemed to reveal an inability to comprehend the plight of European Jewry :

November 16,1938

The new situation in the last few days staggers all belief. I do not know that any words of mine would be useful or can give any comfort. I see no way out.

If the German government carries out its threat of collecting one billion marks from the German Jews, of forcing them to repair their own buildings, of requiring them to pay their insurance to the State, it means that the life of any Jew in Germany becomes impossible. They have all been reduced to starvation and since the Nazi government has shown a reasonable - though not too great tenderness - for human life, they may not allow them to starve but put them in forced labor, or what are politically called labor camps.

I know too that the American members of the Evian conference have been called by the President and are in Washington now....It is nevertheless humanly impossible in my opinion to remove five hundred thousand or more people in a few months.

I think the Jews of Germany should refuse to pay this "fine" because the payment of that fine will be an acceptance of the responsibility for the stupid and cowardly assassination by this foolish Jewish boy of a minor German diplomat in Paris.

I also think that not one penny should be contributed by any Jew outside of Germany toward this fine or toward the release of hostages....But to redeem such hostages would simply embolden these kidnappers and bandits.(19)

**Settlement Projects**

In November 1938, Ambassador Joseph P. Kennedy, the U.S. Ambassador to London, suggested a settlement plan whereby 600,000 Jews were to be resettled in sparsely inhabited parts of the world. But the plan was rejected by both the Secretary of State and the President. When such Jewish leaders as Nahum Goldmann and Louis Lipsky spoke with the American Ambassador in London, they discovered him deeply interested in the problems of the Jewish people. Joseph Kennedy seemed convinced that the Intergovernmental Committee discussions had reached a stage where action was most likely, and he did not feel that Palestine should be excluded as a place of refuge. In his report to the Secretary of State on November 14, 1938, Ambassador Joseph P. Kennedy spoke of the attack on the Jewish community in Germany and the indifference of world opinion as reflecting a most critical situation and he recommended that some sort of Presidential initiative be taken. After speaking with representatives from Latin American republics, the British Dominions and various colonial empires, he found that the doors were closed to Jews. Some governments were willing to consider admitting refugees if Germany permitted them to take property, but they would not even begin to consider indigent refugees. Kennedy concluded his report by reiterating his conviction "that there can be no real appeasement as long as large numbers of people are kept in fear of their lives and uncertain as to their fates...."(20)

The British were concerned with Kennedy's attitude on the refugee question and British Ambassador Sir Ronald Lindsay went to see Under Secretary of State Sumner Welles to report Britain's willingness to relinquish a portion of its immigration quota to America in favor of the German refugees. The Under Secretary explained that quotas granted by Congress were not the property of the nations to whom they were granted. Ambassador Lindsay was concerned with Kennedy's warning that Anglo-American relations would be prejudiced by the refugee question because the feeling in America against the treatment accorded Jews and Catholics in Germany would become so intense as to provoke even more vehement and widespread criticism in America against the policy of appeasement being pursued by Mr. Chamberlain. Welles assured the British Ambassador that the U.S. still relied on the Intergovernmental Committee and hoped that Britain would open portions of its dominions or colonies for refugee settlement.(21)

But Ambassador Kennedy continued to press the British for refuge places. In conversation with Malcolm MacDonald the Ambassador from the U.S. asked "why in heaven's name England did not show more interest in intergovernmental relief as she had all the land," and if Britain offered some of it, the Intergovernmental Committee might have something to work with. Kennedy observed that it seemed as if every one was feeling sorry for the Jews, but nobody was offering any solution. The English responded by claiming that they were in fact doing a great deal to help the refugees. Very confidentially, they told him that they were admitting 75 Jews a day, but that they did not want their own people to know for fear that it might cause trouble.(22)

Nahum Goldmann and Louis Lipsky found that the events in Germany had rendered Zionism a "great service" and they were greatly impressed by Kennedy's own determination to bring about British-American cooperation in an effective solution.(23)

Others felt differently about Kennedy. Justice Louis Brandeis wrote to his friend Robert Szold that James MacDonald of the Intergovernmental Committee was "playing with Chamberlain" through the Ambassador. The Justice felt that Kennedy and Chamberlain were giving the Evian project and the Jews "the run-around."(24)

Bernard Baruch, advisor to President Roosevelt, also had a plan for solving the refugee question. According to which, a part of England's African empire would be converted into the United States of Africa and "there would be place for tens of millions, and they would be the best, strongest and most courageous people, because they are anxious to get away from these overrated goose-stepping civilizations of Germany and Italy."(25) Nothing came of his plan because the British were opposed to it.

Many plans of settlement were proposed, but they were only proposals. By December 1938, more than fifty such projects had been devised and investigated, yet the Jews had no place to go. Alaska and the Virgin Islands offered asylum, but President Roosevelt was opposed on the grounds that admission to U.S. territorial possessions represented a circumvention of the quota laws, and because all kinds of "enemy agents" might enter the country by the backdoor. Roosevelt said that he sympathized with the refugees but he refused to "do anything which would conceivably hurt the future of present American citizens." He advised the Jews to seek other places of refuge.(26)

**The Fear of Spies**

The fear of spies became an obsession and the Roosevelt people found it difficult to differentiate between spies and strangers. While the State Department accused the refugees of being Nazi or Communist agents, President Roosevelt in May of 1940, warned against modern "Trojan Horses" filled with "spies, saboteurs and traitors."(27)

> We know of new methods of attack, the Trojan Horse, the fifth column, that betrays a nation unprepared for treachery. Spies saboteurs and traitors are the actors in this new strategy. With all that we must and will deal vigorously.(28)

In June 1940, the President signed the Alien Registration Act which required all aliens over 14 to be registered and fingerprinted. And a "special care" circular was issued by the State Department advising all consular and diplomatic officers to reevaluate all visas and extirpate the so-called subversive elements. No visa was to be issued if there was "any doubt whatsoever concerning the alien." The best interests of the United States had to be considered even if it meant a "drastic reduction" of quotas.(29) The reinforced controls may have kept some spies out of the country, but it enabled unsympathetic consuls to reject Jews who held legitimate visas and tickets.

The fear of spies ran deep as could be seen by the *S.S. Quanza* incident of September 1940. When the ship with its eighty refugee passengers bound for South America entered Norfolk, Virginia harbor to refuel, the President's Advisory Committee suggested that the passengers be permitted to disembark until private organizations could make arrangements for them to reach their final destination. All had Mexican transit visas and some had visas to various Latin American states, but the State Department refused to permit the debarkation, claiming that such action would be against the law since there was no emergency. After much debate, a compromise solution was adopted, permitting those with transit visas to land temporarily so they could make arrangements to move elsewhere. Soon after screening, it was discovered that five of the eighty passengers were qualified to receive emergency visas to the U.S., and pressure was exerted on the State Department to admit them. Breckinridge Long, Assistant Secretary of State in charge of the Visa Division, was so incensed and galled that he brought his complaint directly to the President, "the list of Rabbis has been closed and now it remains for the President's Committee to be curbed..."(30) Breckinridge Long was the fellow who had been so impressed with Mussolini because the dictator had presumably made the Italian trains run on time, and on April 7, 1936, he had written to William E. Dodd, U.S. Ambassador to Germany:

> From a purely objective point of view, I think the suggestions made by Hitler - If they are sincere...afford the biggest, broadest base for discussion made by any European statesman since the World War.(31)

When in 1941, Long wished to convince Roosevelt to impose even stricter visa regulations to protect America from "undesirables" he came armed with reports from the American Ambassador to Moscow, Lawrence Steinhardt.(32) Ambassador Steinhardt, an American Jew, seemed thoroughly convinced that it was not in the interest of the United States to admit East European Jews. He was sure that they would participate in activities inimical to the United States and that they would "serve the interests of foreign powers." He felt that the admission of refugees on a large-scale basis would result in sabotage, the loss of American lives, and that it would cripple the national defense program. East European Jews were "lawless, scheming, defiant," and "the same kind of criminal Jews who crowd our police dockets in New York...." Long subscribed to Steinhardt's descriptions and went a step further. Long felt that Steinhardt was not only right with respect to Russian and Polish Jews, but that his observations could be applied to "the lower level of all slav population..."

Mr. Steinhardt wrote to Long on May 8, 1941, that he was

> ...firmly convinced that the admission of at least some of them is definitely not in the interest of the United States. I am convinced that there are some among them who will engage in activities in the United States inimical to our institutions and that willingly or unwillingly some of them will serve the interests of foreign powers after their arrival in the United States. I feel strongly that under these circumstances, our present policy of admitting so-called refugees on a very large scale is unsound and that before this war comes to an end we may have occasion to regret this so-called humanitarianism which is likely to result in extensive sabotage and the loss of American lives and property and the crippling of our national defense program to the extent that such sabotage may be effective.(33)

When American Jewish leaders approached President Roosevelt and asked him to let more refugees in, the President confronted them with Steinhardt's reports. Once again, Roosevelt maintained that he sympathized with the plight of the refugees, but he rejected "any plan which would allow any organization whether it be Rabbi Wise or MacDonald or William Green to recommend finally that any person abroad whom they had not seen be admitted to this country." Only extremely needy individuals would be admitted, and then only if they would not in any way endanger United States security.(34) That was Roosevelt's policy and that was the essence of America's diplomacy of rescue. Because of such diplomacy, because of the Nazis and because of the division and sluggishness of Jewish leadership some six million Jews were exterminated in Europe.

1. *Foreign Relations of the United States,* October 24, 1933, December 28, 1933, II, 374 ff.
2  *Ibid.,* January 2, 21; February 21, 28, 1935, II, 414-417.
3  F.D.R. to Constituent, Letter February 10, 1936, President's Official File 198a, F.D.R. Library, Hyde Park, New York.
4  *Foreign Relations of the United States,* March 26, 1933, II, 333-334.
5  Stephen S. Wise Memo described the F.D.R. Cabinet meeting of March 18, 1938, Stephen S. Wise Papers, Brandeis University.
6  Minutes President's Advisory Committee on Political Refugees, May 16, 1938, Stephen S. Wise Papers, Brandeis University.
7  *Ibid.*
8  Little came of that Dominican project. In an interview with Rabbi Maurice L. Perlzweig in 1975, I discovered that a few hundred did manage to find refuge there. Probably one reason more Jews did not find

refuge in the Dominican Republic was because American Jewish investors were concerned that they might lose money there. When in November 1939, Lessing Rosenwald, James N. Rosenberg, Mr. Lamport, Mr. Horowitz (representing Mr. Ittleson) - most were from J.D.C. - met with Senors Davila and Pastoriza of the Dominican Republic, their main expressed concern was that their investments there for the refugees would go bad. According to a Department of State Division of European Affairs memorandum, these American Jewish representatives "expressed very definite unwillingness to place large sums on the table, explained that American business as a result of the crisis was very cautious, and said that they would wish an opportunity to have all the facts in hand with regard to a settlement project before subscribing funds." See Document no. 840.48 Refugees/2028, November 18, 1939.

9   Wilson to Secretary of State, Telegram, November 2, 1938, State Department File No. 840.48 Refugees/865; Wilson to Secretary of State, Telegram, December 9, 1938, State Department File No. 840.48 Refugees/1081; Gilbert to the Secretary of State, Report, December 5, 1938 State Department File No. 862.00/3806, National Archives, Washington, D.C.

10   Emanuel Neumann to Rabbi Stephen S. Wise, October 23, 1938, Robert Szold Papers. A word on the Szold Papers. They are a treasure source of information for this period and when I saw them in the 1960s and 1970s they were scattered in different localities. Some were in the Zionist Archives in New York, and others were still in Mr. Szold's home and office. I went through these papers at all the above mentioned locations.

On April 27, 1971, Dr. Neumann sent me a letter concerning my inquiries about his October 23, 1938 letter to Wise. Dr. Neumann maintained: "I was so deeply concerned for the future of European Jews that I felt that a strong and perhaps desperate effort must be made to open up Palestine so that the prospective victims of Hitlerism could get out." And he further asserted that he "always rejected the attempt to draw a sharp line of demarcation between the plight of the Jews and the problem of Palestine. I have always agreed with Herzl who tried to envisage the Jewish problem as a whole. His "Judenstadt" was his answer to the Jewish plight in European countries."

11   *Foreign Relations of the United States,* February 29, 1940, II, 215-218; April 8, 1941, I, 440-442.
On December 1, 1939, Paul Van Zeeland sent F.D.R. a copy of a resettlement plan which provided for non-sectarian industrial and agricultural projects financed on a "strictly business basis...as investors not as dispensers of charity." F.D.R. criticized the plan for its lack of necessary imagination because it lacked "the psychology which is necessary to success." He found that there was no more room for small projects, "the picture should be in terms of a million square miles occupied by a coordinated self-sustaining civilization." Given such large undertakings,

said F.D.R., he could easily raise the necessary funds. *Foreign Relations of the United States,* December 1, 1939, II, 154-155.

12   *Fortune Quarterly Survey,* April, 1939.

13   Memo by Stephen S. Wise, November 14, 1938, Stephen S. Wise Papers, Brandeis University.

14   Memo Division of European Affairs, February 23, 1939, State Department File No. 840.48 Refugees/1488, National Archives, Washington, D.C.

15   Sam Rosenman to Myron Taylor, November 23, 1938, President's Official File 3186, F.D.R. Library, Hyde Park, New York.

16   Newton Jenkins to Cordell Hull, Telegram, March 25, 1938, State Department File No. 840.48 Refugees/15, National Archives, Washington, D.C.

17   *Foreign Relations of the United States,* November 14, 1938, II, 396-398.

18   Stephen S.Wise Memo, December 2, 1938, Stephen S., Wise Papers, Brandeis University; F.D.R. to Harold Ickes, December 18, 1940, F.D.R. Papers, F.D.R. Library, Hyde Park, New York.

19   Cyrus Adler to Neville Laski, November 16, 1938, Cyrus Adler Papers, Congress House, New York City.

20   Joseph P. Kennedy to Secretary of State, Telegram, November 14, 1938, State Department File No. 840.48 Refugees/896, National Archives, Washington, D.C.

21   Memo of conversation between Sir Ronald Lindsay and Under Secretary of State, November 17, 1938, State Department File No. 840.48 Refugees/911½, National Archives, Washington, D.C.

22   Joseph P. Kennedy to Secretary of State, Telegram, November 18, 1938, State Department File No. 840.48 Refugees/916 National Archives, Washington, D.C.

23   Nahum Goldmann and Louis Lipsky to Louis D. Brandeis, November 17, 1938, Robert Szold Papers.

24   Louis D. Brandeis to Robert Szold, November 17, 1938, Robert Szold Papers.

25   Bernard Baruch Memo, January 24, 1939, Bernard Baruch Papers Princeton University Library.

In the Jewish Agency Papers I found a note of "X's" Report on his/her interview with Mr. Joseph P. Kennedy, Tuesday, November 2, 1938, 11 A.M. Ambassador Kennedy said that the two things he had to worry about in London were "the Jewish question and trade agreements" and he was keeping in close touch with the Palestine problem. "As a Catholic in Boston he had reason to know what discrimination meant; his own father had been unable to find any entree in Boston, and he had eventually been forced to look elsewhere for a livilhood. But for the Jews, the proposition was a hundred times worse." He did not feel that the "President, as a Protestant could feel about the Jewish question in the same way as he Kennedy, felt about it." Then Kennedy asked Mr. or Ms. X

16    The Doors Were Closed

what he or she would think if he were to visit Hitler to discuss the Jewish question. X replied that he had heard this subject was an "obsession with Hitler, so that he became virtually insane when it was raised." But Kennedy said that he nevertheless had "more than half a mind to pay him such a visit. It might light a few bonfires in the United States, but all the same he was tempted to intervene." - From a Secret Memo dated November 2, 1938, Jewish Agency Papers, Zionist Archives, New York.

26   In August 1940, Lawrence Cramer, Governor of the Virgin Islands agreed to open his territory to refugee settlement. But the State Department interceded to stop his proposal. B. Long presented his case directly to F.D.R. He claimed that the refugees would be flouting U.S. laws, that they would be sneaking into America by the back door and that all kinds of undesirables and spies would enter. The President accepted Long's arguments and suggested that areas without serious economic and social problems should be found for the refugees. Said F.D.R.: "I have sympathy, I cannot, however, do anything which would conceivably hurt the future of present American citizens." F.D.R. to Harold Ickes, President's Official File 3186, December 18, 1940, F.D.R. Papers, F.D.R. Library, Hyde Park, New York.

27   *New York Times,* May 26, 1940

28   *Ibid.*

29   *Foreign Relations of the United States,* June 5, 29, 1940, II, 229-232.

30   B. Long Memo, September 5, 1940, B. Long Papers, The Library of Congress.

31   B. Long to William E. Dodd, April 7, 1936, William E. Dodd Papers, The Library of Congress.

32   In an interview with Dr. Emanuel Neumann of the Jewish Agency, I discovered that Steinhardt had been a great disappointment to the Jewish community of America. He and such groups as the American Jewish Committee had helped add to the State Department's opposition to Erez Israel becoming once again the Jewish Homeland. Interview with Dr. Neumann, May 6, 1971.

33   Steinhardt to Long, May 8, 1941, B. Long Papers, The Library of Congress. See also B. Long's memo dated September 5, 1940, B. Long Papers, and B. Long Diary of November 27, 1941.
On January 13, 1944, Nahum Goldmann would praise Steinhardt in a letter to Long: "We all know what great services Ambassador Steinhardt has rendered in the past and is still rendering to the suffering Jews of Europe." N. Goldmann to B. Long, January 13, 1944, Department of State File No. 840.48 Refugees/5010, National Archives, Washington, D.C. Could Goldmann have been trying to win friends and influence people through such letters? Could it be that he was being cynical?

34   B. Long Diary, October 10, 1940, Library of Congress; Minutes President's Advisory Committee on Political Refugees, October 30, 1940, Stephen S. Wise Papers, Brandeis University Library.

# CHAPTER II

## Seas of Indifference

The *St. Louis* was one of many ships that sailed in the seas of indifference. She and her Jewish passengers were the victims of indifferent governments, corrupt officialdom, closed doors and Jewish organizations that were too slow to act, and were more concerned with money than with European Jewry. The tribulations of the refugees on board the *St. Louis* symbolized the fate of six million Jews of Europe.

The *St. Louis* was one of many ships that sailed from European ports with refugee passengers headed for safe shores. But as more and more Jews sought safety the entry price to safe havens rose higher and higher while more and more doors were closed.

The passengers on board the *St. Louis* - a ship headed for Cuba - had paid for their $150 tourist visa fee, but they would not reach their destination. They soon found themselves entangled in the midst of Cuban political intrigue, U.S. official indifference and lentatudinous Jewish American leadership.

President Laredo Bru of Cuba, representing the civil servants, was in conflict with Benitez, Chief of the Immigration Department, who represented the military faction of Cuba. Benitez had successfully pocketed a tidy sum while helping refugees enter Cuba with tourist visas, which were subject to question by the authorities only if the refugees decided to stay in Cuba.

While the Joint Distribution Committee took an active interest in the welfare of the Jewish European refugees, and contributed money for their benefit, some of its leadership was so inept in dealing with the Cubans and so provincially stingy that Cuba became closed as a place of refuge. Cuba, like most nations at the time, was concerned with what Cuba might get by helping the refugees. The U.S. refused to intervene on behalf of the refugees and it failed even to consider to let them stay in the Panama Canal Zone area on a temporary basis. This despite the fact that 743 of the *St. Louis'* passengers had U.S. quota numbers and could legally enter the U.S. from within three months to three years after their arrival in Cuba.

The *St. Louis* affair together with thousands of similar acts of indifference committed by the so-called freedom loving nations and peoples from 1933 to 1945, indicated to the German Government that the world did not care as to what might happen to the Jews. They saw that at times even certain influential Jews did not care as to what might happen to the Jews.

On May 8, 1939, the High Commissioner for Refugees - Lord Duncanan - advised Jewish organizations in Europe against sending the refugees on board the *St. Louis* to Cuba. He warned that there would be great difficulties ahead for the passengers "in regard to their entry into Cuba and (he) strongly urged that the refugees should not be sent there."(1) But on May 13, 1939, the *St. Louis* sailed even though Jewish organizations that sponsored the journey were well aware that there might be trouble ahead. Since the world was indifferent to the plight of the refugees, and the doors of refuge were closed, they felt that they had to use shock tactics to awaken the world to its base indifference.(2)

But soon those very organizations and their leadership would feel that they had made a mistake.

President Bru ordered the Cuban Immigration Department not to clear the ship; not even to go on board to find out if there were people with visas, bonds or landing permits. The *St. Louis* was not even permitted to remain at the dock. She was ordered to pull out into the basin with police guards around her.

A representative of the Joint Distribution Committee (Mr. Goldsmith) went to see President Bru, but the Cuban President said that he did not wish to let them land because he feared anti-Semitic riots in Havana. Goldsmith was not impressed by Bru's fabrications, and he warned him that it would not improve Cuba's image if he kept the refugees from landing after they had provided Cuban authorities with large sums of money. Goldsmith's arguments did not move Bru. He wanted more money.

Goldsmith then went to du Bois, the American Consul, and asked him to intervene, but du Bois refused. The official American position was that it could not ask the Cubans to permit the Jews to land in Cuba when the U.S. would not permit them in the United States.

Word was received by the Jewish organizations that the Cubans would not allow the immigrants to disembark since the ship had sailed more than 24 hours after President Bru's May 6th decree, which required refugees to carry visas approved by the Cuban State, Labor and Treasury departments. The J.D.C.'s New York office became concerned that there would be more "ghost ships" sailing the seas unless someone, somewhere "kicked in" with plenty of money before the ships were due in Havana.(3)

J.D.C. representatives in Havana were greatly bewildered by the inaction of their superiors in New York. While Cuban authorities were making a house to house search for Jews in Havana, and while there was talk of pogroms against the Jews, they had no instructions. Goldsmith in Havana urgently telephoned Lawrence Berenson, a lawyer associated with the J.D.C. who at one time headed the Cuban Chamber of Commerce in the U.S. "Why," asked Goldsmith, "hasn't anyone come from New York? We are forced to sit here in Havana with our hands tied, with no authority to act. The *St. Louis* will probably not be permitted to unload its passengers. Send someone or give us some authority to act. We need some authority to act. The people in Havana are deliberately looking for trouble. The passengers on board those ships are panic-stricken, something must be done."(4)

Berenson said he would come down to Havana and speak to Benitez and Colonel Batista, but that was all he said.(5)

On the 26th of May, the *St. Louis* arrived with 943 passengers. Some 900 had temporary landing permits.(6) While such State Department officials as Under Secretary of State Sumner Welles were opposed to making any sort of representations to the Cuban Government on behalf of the refugees,(7) Jewish leaders of the J.D.C. were likewise unwilling to do their utmost to help their fellow Jews. During their June 1, 1939 meeting, the J.D.C. leadership heard James N. Rosenberg denounce the pressure tactics of the Cuban regime and declare his opposition to giving the Cuban President the money he wanted. Money seemed more important than lives. But that was understandable since such individuals were comfortably situated in America, and they were not on board such ships as the *St. Louis*, in desperate need of help.

"It seems to me unthinkable," said Rosenberg, "for the J.D.C. to give a blank check in perpetuity for these people." He maintained that the "J.D.C. cannot assume more than a short term obligation," and "the maximum obligation which the J.D.C. could assume would be one year, a quarter of a million dollars."

Jaretzki agreed that a large sum of money should not be provided and he carried that line of thought a step further by insisting that "if we went down and allowed some kind of guarantee there would immediately be some other ships following. There is no limit to what you let yourself in for. It is a horrible thing, but almost necessary in order to prevent the continued shipment of what we must characterize as illegal immigrants."(8)

Rosenberg chimed in that every time the J.D.C. did something like this it was encouraging the German Government to kick out its Jews. He recalled that in previous instances, the J.D.C. had decided it was not "going to be held up by this policy of forced shipment of unfortunate people by Germany." He regarded it as part of a Nazi German plot to "send unfortunate people who cannot support themselves to places where they are not wanted and then having those people seem poor, penniless, useless persons (because they can't work) and make them the nucleus for spreading anti-Semitism into every quarter of the world. We must try to view these very difficult problems without letting our hearts run away with us." He then suggested that the 110 children on board be given a chance to land with a J.D.C. guarantee of $60,000 a year for three years. "I recognize particularly the tragic prospect of separating young children from their parents, but it is better for the parent that the child should have a chance of life than they should be driven back to destruction."(9)

Henry Ittleson's observations summed up the capability of such organizations as the J.D.C. when, during that June 1 meeting, he said that "we can only aid in an interim way, not in mass settlement. This I consider mass resettlement. We have no facilities for that."(10)

A thousand people was "mass resettlement" for some. They could not afford to help a thousand Jews. They could not afford to act quickly to help a thousand of their brethren, and so Cuba as a place of refuge soon was closed to Europe's Jews. They could not afford to help a thousand of their Brethren?

But while some organizational leaders were tight fisted, the general public reaction was overwhelmingly generous. Writing to his Congressman, Abraham Zucca of Miami, Florida, offered his apartment to four refugees. Zucca even promised to provide his four refugees with food for as long as they needed it and he was sure that he could "sign up three or four hundred Miamians to do the same."(11) There were hundreds of offers made by such individuals.

There was no shortage of money. There was just a shortage of goodwill and good sense.

All other considerations aside, the people on board the *St. Louis* were people who would never have become burdens to society. Many were professionals and most were hard working families. Any society should have been happy to receive them. The Rosenbergs, Brus and Roosevelts were as wrong as they could have been in their fear that the refugees would become burdensome.

**May 31:** President Bru said that the Hamburg Line had to be taught a lesson since it brought passengers with documents obtained through bribery. He expressed sympathy for the refugees, but he wanted them sent back. (12)

**June 1:** Lawrence Berenson had an interview with President Bru and obtained a promise from him that as soon as the *St. Louis* was outside the 12 mile territorial limit he would listen to any plan of guarantees covering the maintenance of the refugees in Cuba until such time as they could go elsewhere. Berenson was convinced that President Bru would permit the refugees to remain in Cuba. (13)

**June 2:** The *St. Louis* set sail for Hamburg, Germany. Captain Schroeder told the passengers that he would delay at sea as much as possible. The money which the passengers had given Cuban officials for the tourist visas was not returned.

**June 3:** The J.D.C. wired its sister organizations in Europe not to encourage any further emigration of Jews from Europe unless the people had legitimate papers:

> We deem vital every effort be made to discourage all steamship agencies, bureaus, etc. from selling passage or from leading refugees hope they may be admitted except only when there is absolute certainty visas issued and all other legal

requirements complied with to satisfaction of central governments.(14)

**June 4:** President Bru told Berenson the terms for permitting the passengers to land. Five hundred dollars for each in cash deposit, plus full maintenance guarantees. Total sum nearly $1,000,000. If this sum could be provided within 48 hours the refugees could land.

Finally the J.D.C. officials in New York urged that every possible sacrifice must be made to prevent a return of the refugees to Germany. Rosenberg's June 6 answer was that "such forced immigration must never again be put on our shoulders," but he offered a loan of one thousand dollars to the J.D.C. if 500 men throughout the country would do likewise.(15)

It was too late. The June 6 deadline had come and gone. Berenson, the J.D.C. representative in Cuba, had tried to outdo President Bru in horse-trading instead of trying to save the lives of the people on board the *St. Louis*. Agreement had been reached to land the exiles for $500 in cash guarantees for each, but Berenson went back on his agreement and proposed a $443,000 guarantee for those on board the *St. Louis* and the 150 additional refugees aboard the steamers *Orduna* and *Flandres*.(16) This (Berenson's) sum was to include expenses for feeding and lodging of the refugees. The Cubans rejected Berenson's offer.(17)

Berenson was distraught by what he considered a personal defeat. He told the American Consul in Havana that the Cuban officials had been after graft amounting to $500,000. He also complained that New York J.D.C. officials had annoyed him with telephone calls urging him to meet Bru's full demands, but he had insisted that he could save them a considerable amount of money.(18)

On June 6, the U.S. Department of State informed du Bois that the Chase National Bank, representing leading financiers in New York, was empowered to give the Cuban government "whatever sums were considered necessary" to permit the people to land. But the American Consul was still advised that under no circumstances should an American official intervene "in the matter of the landing of the *St. Louis* passengers or of any other passenger refugees." Avra M. Warren, of the Visa Division, with backing from the Secretary of State and the President, repeated those instructions twice and made du Bois repeat them back to him." (19)

J.D.C. officials worried about the consequences to the prestige of their organization if the *St. Louis* were forced back to Germany. Ed Kaufman, of J.D.C., telegraphed James N. Rosenberg on June 7, and pleaded with him for a more reasonable and humane approach:

> If our organization, particularly J.D.C. and coordinating committee, permits the *St. Louis* to return to Germany with its cargo of human misery, it will definitely affect fund-raising next year.
>
> We are dealing in human beings and it is no disgrace nor defeat to make a bad bargain under the circumstances. Human life has greater value than dollars.(20)

Yet in the midst of the *St. Louis* tragedy, James M. Rosenberg telegraphed Paul Baerwald of his concern for the money it might cost the Jewish community to save the Jews:

> June 8, 1939
>
> J.D.C. approved $500,000 toward foundation provided British will put in their $500,000 and provided nothing is done to shift to the shoulders of the Jews largescale immigration projects which require government help. I now understand from Lewis that British are saying to you that America must go forward and in principle agree to astronomical amounts to be furnished to foundation for settlement purposes.
>
> Do not let yourself be swamped by any such position.
>
> Burden is not on private funds but on Governments.
>
> You representing America are doing your share. If Britain refuses to do its share let the record be clear that we have done ours and they have failed.
>
> Stick to this position like grim death and whatever the outcome you and J.D.C. have not failed in this great issue.(21)

After having received his instructions the American Ambassador to Cuba went to see President Bru to tell him that the money he had requested was available. But the American intervention was too late. Bru replied courteously, but firmly, that the *St. Louis* matter should be considered closed. He was willing, however, to discuss the matter of refugees on other ships. All refugees had to fulfill entrance requirements stipulated by Cuban laws.(22)

As far as Cuba was concerned, the *St. Louis* matter was closed, and Cuba would no longer be a place of refuge for the Jews despite Bru's declared willingness to consider letting in other refugees.

On June 8th, the captain on board the *St. Louis* cabled:

> Proceding directly to Germany. Will no doubt cause panic.
> We have taken counter measures.
> Think that we shall be successful but all consequences are absolutely very unpleasant.(23)

### A Mother's Courage

On June 6, 1939, the Daily Mirror of New York published a letter from a mother on board the *St. Louis* to her children. The letter was dated May 31, 1939.

> It is so strange how near, and yet how much cut off we really are. Because many boats come close to us throughout the day bringing greetings from relatives and friends, many millions of rumors are gossipped on the boat. The result is that two-thirds of the passengers are absolutely panicky. I am not one of them.
>
> I am trying to be courageous; I help others with encouragement. I feel that you are backing me from far away, and that gives me courage to go on.(24)

### In Search of a Place

Ambassador Joseph P. Kennedy spoke to the French and British authorities about the possibility of accepting the *St. Louis* refugees by Britain and France. The British said no at first. They refused to admit the refugees under such pressure because it would create a precedent for Palestine where Jewish organizations working with German and Italian shipping lines were trying to force their hand. The British would consider admitting the *St. Louis* passengers only after they returned to Germany and after the British Cabinet gave its approval. The French said they might take on the children and make arrangements for a limited number of adults to land in Morocco.(25)

As the J.D.C. promised to guarantee for the maintenance and emigration of the *St. Louis* people, the British agreed to consider admitting 300 of the passengers if Belgium, Holland and France took their share. Ambassador Kennedy then joined the private organizations in making further inquiries with France, Holland

and Belgium. The British proposed that the United States join in a declaration protesting against Germany's forcing German Jews to emigrate without legitimate papers, and that places of refuge would not be found for people being forced to emigrate in that way.(26) In other words, the British were prepared once more to advise Germany that the West did not want those Jews.

On June 14, Kennedy reported that arrangements had been completed for the *St. Louis* passengers to proceed to Antwerp, Belgium where the selection of various contingents would be made:

> The Belgium and Netherlands contingents will be disembarked and the French and British contingents transferred by tender to a smaller vessel of the Hamburg Amerika Line which will take them to a French and British port at the expense of the line.(27)

The *St. Louis* tragedy tells the story of the six million and the diplomacy of rescue. The passengers could have found refuge in Cuba. There was room, but bureaucracy prevented it. In Cuba, it was the bureaucracy of an indifferent government. As far as the Jews of America and their organizations were concerned, they were weak, badly disunited, and afraid because of their own uncertain positions and the growing influence of the Nazis. When some action was taken, it was too little and too late.

From the early 1930s until January 1944, there was lots of talk of rescue. Jewish organizations such as the J.D.C. apparently invested money to help European Jewry,(28) but those sums were far too insignificant in terms of the needs. Strikes, demonstrations - ACTION - against Nazi German atrocities and indifferent governments was not there. As Nahum Goldmann put it in his autobiography:

> If we had succeeded in the first few years in organizing an effective anti-Nazi boycott and mobilizing the influence of Jews, especially in America and England, against the Nazi regime when it was still weak and if...millions of gentiles would have joined us, we might have produced, if not the suspension of the Nuremberg Laws, at least a mitigation of the persecution and possibly an arrangement whereby German Jews could emigrate ...But all these proposals met with very little response in the world and...they were actually opposed by influential Jews in the United States.(29)

In January 1944, the U.S. established the War Refugee Board to help rescue Europe's remaining Jewish population. The W.R.B. was still one more bureaucratic organization. While it did help save a few Jews, it failed to provide these Jews with a place to go. America and the "free" world remained closed to Jews.

1 Lord Duncanan to President HIAS-ICA Immigration Association, Paris, May 8, 1939, Joint Distribution Committee Papers, New York. Hereafter cited as J.D.C. Papers.
2 Ambassador Joseph P. Kennedy to Secretary of Sate, June 10, 1939 State Department File No. 837.55J/54, National Archives, Washington, D.C.
3 Margolis to Razovsky, May 23, 1939, J.D.C. Papers.
4 Conference Call, May 25, 1939, J.D.C. Papers.
5 *Ibid.*
6 The *SS Orduna* pulled into the harbor and the *SS Flandres* was expected the next day.
7 Memo by du Bois, May 29, 1939, State Department File No. 837.55J, National Archives, Washington, D.C.
8 J.D.C. meeting June 1, 1939 minutes, J.D.C. Papers.
9 *Ibid.*
10 *Ibid.*
11 Letters from Americans to U.S. Government regarding the *St. Louis*, State Department File No. 837.55J/45, National Archives, Washington, D.C.
12 du Bois to Secretary of State, May 31, 1939, State Department File No. 837.55J/39, National Archives, Washington, D.C.
13 *Ibid.* June 1, 1939.
14 J.D.C. to agencies in Europe, Telegram, June 3, 1939, J.D.C. Papers.
15 J.D.C. Papers.
16 *Ibid.*
17 Jewish Telegraphic Agency Report, June 6, 1939.

18  du Bois to Secretary of State, June 6, 1939, Department of State File No. 837.55J/39, National Archives, Washington, D.C.
19  *Ibid.*
20  J.D.C. Papers.
21  *Ibid.*
22  Ambassador to Secretary of State, June 8, 1939, Department of State File No. 837.55J/43, National Archives, Washington, D.C.
23  J.D.C. Papers.
24  *The Daily Mirror,* June 16, 1939.
25  Ambassador Kennedy to Secretary of State, June 10, 1939, Department of State File No. 837.55J/54, National Archives, Washington, D.C.  26  Ambassador Kennedy to Secretary of State, June 12, 1939, State Department File No. 837.55J/53. National Archives, Washington, D.C.
27  *Ibid.,* June 14, 1939, State Department File No 837.55J/50, National Archives, Washington, D.C.
28  Oscar Handlin, *A Continuing Task, The American Jewish Joint Distribution Committee, 1914-1964* (New York, 1964), 62-89.
29  *The Autobiography of Nahum Goldmann, Sixty Years of Jewish Life* translated by Helen Sebba (New York, 1969) 147-148.

# CHAPTER III
# Speak Not for the Jews Are Burning

On March 17, 1943, the Jewish National Committee, representing the fighting Jews in Poland wrote to Rabbi Stephen S. Wise, Nahum Goldmann and the Joint Distribution Committee:

> This is to report to you the most dreadful crime of all times - the mass murder of millions of Jews in Poland. In the face of the acute danger that the still surviving Jews will be exterminated we appeal to you:
> 1. For vengeance on the Germans.
> 2. To force the Hitlerites to cease their murder.
> 3. To fight for our life and our honor.
> 4. For contact with neutral countries.
> 5. To save 10,000 of our children by means of exchange.
>
> The remnants of Jewish communities in Poland exist in the conviction that during these most troubled days of our history you have not brought us help. Respond at least now in the last days of our life. This is our final appeal to you.

On November 15, 1943, the Jewish National Committee, representing some of the Jews fighting in Poland wrote to Dr. Schwarzbart in London of their fight against the Nazis:

> We write you with the blood in which tens of thousands of our Jewish martyrs are perishing. We are now living through the Epilogue of our terrible tragedy. The Nazi barbarians in the face of their defeat are murdering off the pitiful remnants of the Jewish population.
>
> Last month we estimated that there were only between 250 - 300,000 Jews left in Poland. It is our opinion that in a few weeks there will only remain about 50,000.
>
> During their dying moments, the remnants of Jews in Poland cried out to the world begging for help.
>
> We know that you are with us heart and soul and that you experience deeply our martyrdom which is unexampled in history. We also know that you are powerless. But let those circles who could have helped us at least know what we think of them!
>
> The blood of 3,000,000 Polish Jews will take revenge not only

against the Nazi murderers, but against those indifferent elements which have contented themselves merely with words but have done nothing to rescue from the hands of the beasts a people doomed to extermination. This we...can never forget or forgive.

May this - possibly the final cry from the depths - reach the ears of the world.

We want all Jews, and the world at large, to know that our youth nobly defended the life and the honor of its people. Since the heroic epic of the Warsaw Ghetto we have written in recent months the grand and glorious chapter of the Jews of Bialystok.

Just as in Warsaw, the Germans entered the ghetto on armored trucks and equipped with field artillery. They brought along about 1,000 gendarmes and SS-men and a number of Ukrainian detachments.

The Jews retaliated mostly with grenades and incendiary bombs, they also had a few machine guns. They fought with frantic determination which roused the admiration of the population of the city and the district. Several hundred Germans and Ukrainians fell or were wounded during the battle.

In order to crush the uprising the Germans did what they had done in Warsaw - they set the ghetto afire. The bitter fighting lasted 8 days. But the Jewish resistances did not weaken and lasted for another month, into the middle of September. The heroic battle in Bialystok will share its place in history with the resistance of Warsaw.

During the last few months, the Jews have engaged in two other uprisings which were of great symbolic importance. They destroyed two extermination centers - the death camps at Treblinka...and Sobibor (in the District of Chelm-Lubin). At both camps the remnants of the Jewish victims who were awaiting death organized in fighting "fives" and at a pre-arranged moment, launched their attack; throwing themselves fiercely upon the German and Ukrainian guards, they disarmed and killed the majority of them, burned down the gas chambers and the "living crematoria" and after having accomplished this, escaped to the neighboring forests.

But the Jews resisted not only in Warsaw, Bialystok, Treblinka and Sobibor. Similar organized uprisings took place in Czestechowa, Bendzin, Wilno, Tarnow and in a number of small localities.

Our sufferings you can neither understand nor conceive. In order to understand them you, who are in London and Tel Aviv, would have to be possessed of diseased imaginations. All the centers of Jewish life have been erased from the earth. Their inhabitants met death in the torture centers of Treblinka, Sobibor, Belzec and Oscwiecim.

In order that there may remain a mark after those who died with their weapons in their hands, fighting against the enemy, we write you these lines....

As you read our letter, do not for a moment think that we are broken of spirit or have fallen victims to resignation. We regard our merciless doom with sober eyes. We know you have done everything possible to save us. It is easier for us to die knowing that freedom will come to the world and believing that Palestine will become the Fatherland of the Jewish Nation.

Yours,

November 15, 1943                    Cwja, Icchak (1)

There were many communications and pleas sent by the Jews of Nazi occupied Europe to the outside world. How did the world respond? As Dr. Nahum Goldmann and Rabbi Stephen S. Wise recalled, the world failed to respond. In his autobiography, Goldmann wrote:

We must stand as a generation not only condemned to witness the destruction of a third of our number but guilty of having accepted it without any resistance worthy of the name.(2)

And as Rabbi Stephen S. Wise wrote to his friend the Reverend John Hanes Holmes:

This war against us began before there was war...and if you and I...and any of us, who had some spiritual and moral power, had moved America and Britain and France really to intervene on behalf of the slain innocents war might not have come.(3)

If Rabbi Wise's and Dr. Goldmann's observations were germane to the 1930s they were more so in the terrible 1940-1945 period, when the world ignored the atrocities being committed against the Jews and thereby abetted the German "final solution." The Allies appeared willing to see the Jews exterminated, for it saved them from the embarassment of not sheltering the Jews. They collaborated in a conspiracy of silence, ignoring and sometimes suppressing atrocity reports because they feared public demands for the relaxation of immigration restrictions.

In the summer of 1942, after Rabbi Stephen S. Wise received detailed reports from Gerhard Riegner (a German Jew who had fled to Geneva, Switzerland, and there represented the World Jewish Congress) of how millions of Jews had been slaughtered by the Germans and of how millions more would be killed unless the Allies took direct and immediate action, he asked the State Department to confirm the accounts, advise the President and pursue whatever steps it deemed advisable.

The State Department requested Rabbi Wise to keep the reports secret until they could be verified, and at first he complied. According to a report Nahum Goldmann gave the War Emergency Conference of the World Jewish Congress in November 1944, Jewish officials followed Under Secretary of State Sumner Welles' instructions that the atrocity reports not be released until they had been checked with the Vatican because they wanted to keep the Geneva lines of communication open. If the atrocity reports had been published without State Department approval, said Goldmann, that would have been "the last telegram" they would have received from Geneva.(4) This was a strange argument since Rabbi Wise and the American branch of the World Jewish Congress had not received its information directly from Geneva, but through the London office of that organization. According to Dr. Riegner, he sent the reports to London and New York because he was afraid that somewhere along the line someone might try to suppress the information.(5) This leads to the question as to how the information came into Riegner's possession.

The reports of mass extermination came to Riegner's attention through Benjamin Sagalowitz, Press Secretary to the Federation of Swiss Jewish Communities. Sagalowitz had been alerted to the situation by a business friend of the German Ambassador to Switzerland, and he immediately got in touch with Riegner. Riegner and Sagalowitz then met with the German businessman. The man's reliability was investigated and the truth of his stories was ascertained. "No one really believed that the human mind was capable of doing such things," said Riegner.(6) But there were some decisive factors that made Riegner believe the stories. On the 15th of July there had been mass arrests in the streets of Holland, Belgium, France and elsewhere. The atrocity reports following so closely the mass arrests meant that the Nazis had decided on a policy of total extermination. The second factor was that Riegner had seen how brutal the Germans could be when he lived in Germany in the late 1920s and early 1930s. And finally, the speeches of Hitler and Goering pointed in the direction of the extermination policy.(7)

Riegner went to the British and American representatives in Switzerland and asked them to inform their governments, verify the facts, and transmit the information to Rabbi Stephen S. Wise in New York and to Sydney Silverman in London. In the text to Silverman he added the words "inform New York." Wise "did not get the report directly," according to Riegner, "because it was suppressed by the American State Department."(8)

According to Riegner, his October 1942 encounter with the American Minister, Leland Harrison, was "unforgettable." Harrison had asked Riegner to submit all the evidence he could gather and Riegner presented him with a thirty page document. Among the documentation were eye-witness accounts from two individuals who had escaped from the jaws of death. One witness was a young Jew from Latvia who had seen the extermination of the Jews in the city of Riga.

The young Jew escaped and finally got to Switzerland where he had some distant relatives. Riegner questioned him for many hours. The second witness was a Polish Jew, a mechanic, who had been arrested during the mass arrests in Belgium, and was deported to the region near Stalingrad. He worked near the German fortifications there. When a German officer needed a mechanic and a driver, he volunteered. The Jew told the German what the extermination policy was all about: "Those who could work were put to work, the others were murdered." The German officer was apparently fed up with the war since he had lost two of his brothers and he decided to help this Jew escape. He provided the Jew with food and occupation money and hid him on a train loaded with uniforms which went from Stalingrad to Paris. Riegner questioned the man for some nine hours.(9) Harrison read the document for over half an hour without saying a word. When he had finished he started over again, this time he questioned Riegner page by page. What puzzled Riegner was that Harrison had not shown "any emotion whatsoever."(10)

Because of the importance of the documents obtained by the World Jewish Congress, I feel I must include them in full. What follows is the document received by Rabbi Maurice L. Perlzweig, Chairman, British Section of the World Jewish Congress:

World Jewish Congress
Geneva Office
Note regarding Hitler's instruction
concerning the annihilation of the Jews
in Europe.

-------------------------------------------------------------------------------

1. In the first days of August 1942 the Geneva Office of the World Jewish Congress received an information from a reliable German source, to the effect that in the Furhrer's Head-Quarters a plan had been discussed according to which the total of the Jews living in Germany and German occupied and controlled countries, numbering from three and a half to four million, should - after having been deported and concentrated in certain regions of Eastern Europe - be exterminated by one stroke, in order to solve once for all the Jewish question in Europe. This action was reported as having been planned for the autumn of 1942. The ways and means how this plan should be executed, were still under consideration.

2. On August 8, the Geneva Office of the World Jewish Congress submitted the above information to His Majesty's Consul in Geneva, asking him
   a. that the British Government should be informed without delay.
   b. that the competent Services of the British Government be requested to make investigations as to the reliability of this information and
   c that the Chairman of the British Section of the World Jewish Congress, Mr. Sydney S. Silverman, M.P. in London should simultaneously be informed of the situation.

3. His Majesty's Consul in Geneva kindly agreed to comply with this request. On September 1st, the Chairman of the British Section of the World Jewish Congress informed the Geneva Office of the World Jewish Congress by cable that the above message had reached him.
Meanwhile the substance of the above mentioned information has been confirmed by the fact that large deportations have taken place in nearly all European countries as well as by various reports received concerning mass executions of Jews. A further confirmation was given by Hitler himself in his last speech of September 30, in the Sport-Palast in Berlin.
The Geneva Office of the World Jewish Congress is now in

a position to implement its previous information by the following details.

In addition to its first report the above mentioned German source has now stated that the plan to exterminate the Jews of Europe, which in the second half of July was still under discussion in the Fuhrer's Head-Quarters, has meanwhile become a reality by an order issued by the Fuhrer. The draft-project had been submitted to Hitler by Herman BACKE, Secretary of State for Economics. Mr. Backe is said to have based the plan on economic reasons, as the difficult food situation would be eased by the annihilation of about four million persons who otherwise would have to be fed.

Although the anti-Jewish policy has always been one of the main points of the National-Socialist program, an important section of the Party was for various reasons opposed to Mr. Backe's plan. In the first place Dr. Frank, Governor General of the occupied Polish territories, who about the same time ceased to be a minister of the Reich, opposed the plan on different economic reasons. He drew attention to the shortage of labour in the General-gouvernement and the East of Europe generally; he declared that large numbers of Jews in the eastern countries were artisans or specialized in other industrial callings particularly needed and lacking in Poland. In spite of this opposition the plan submitted by Mr. Backe was accepted by Hitler, and at the end of July the Fuhrer signed an order according to which all European Jews on whom the Germans could lay hands, should be deported to Eastern Europe and should be destroyed.

Our German informer assures us that he himself saw this order at the Fuhrer's Head-Quarters.

Our informer has for a long time been known to several persons in Switzerland in close contact with us, as being a man of highest standard of perfect reliability. He is a prominent German industrialist and belongs to the inner circle of advisors about war-economy to the German Government. He has access to the Fuhrer's Head-Quarters. He is known to be opposed to the Nazi-system and when disclosing the first information at the beginning in August, he stated that he had left Germany for the special reason of informing the outside world in order to facilitate any possible counter-measures. It should also be recalled that during his visit at the beginning of August he reported about the replacement of Field-Marshall von Bock, which had taken place about two weeks prior to his arrival here, an information which later proved to be correct.

Also other information coming from the same source has subsequently been confirmed by events.(11)

In October 1942, the Jewish Telegraphic Agency publicized the atrocity reports even though the State Department did not lift its restrictions until it had received four sworn statements verifying the Riegner reports a month later.

In response to public demand for action, the Allies issued a declaration on December 17, 1942, denouncing the atrocities and they pledged to punish the guilty, but they still did not find it possible to mention the Jews as the victims. In their December declaration, Belgium, Czechoslovakia, France, Greece, Luxembourg, the Netherlands, Norway, Poland, Russia, Great Britain, the U.S.A. and Yugoslavia condemned "in the strongest possible terms this bestial policy of cold-blooded extermination." They declared that such events could only strengthen "the resolve of all freedom loving peoples to overthrow the barbarous Hitlerite tyranny." And they reaffirmed their "solemn resolution to ensure that those responsible for those crimes shall not escape retribution and to press on with the necessary practical measures to this end."(12)

Such pronouncements in no way persuaded the Nazis to discontinue their program of extermination for on January 21, 1943, Riegner reported that every day some 6,000 Jews were being murdered.(13)

Author Ben Hecht telegraphed the President and wondered why the Allies failed to mention Jews in their declaration against Nazi atrocities.

...there is not one word about the slaughter of more than two million Jewish men, women and children. That this, the darkest crime in all the annals of history, is not mentioned specifically and stressed in a statement of Nazi atrocities, must be considered as a fatal oversight or else a grave injustice, not only to the Jewish people but to humanity iteslf.

We must urgently and solemnly request in the name of humanity and justice, that a specific statement by you, Mr. President, Prime Minister Churchill and Premier Stalin, be issued in the condemnation of Nazi Germany's crimes against the Jewish people of Europe which will make it clear beyond any doubt that for these crimes, too, they will be punished with equal severity.(14)

American Jewish leaders once again turned to President Roosevelt for assistance. In December, Rabbi Wise wrote him that as many as two million Jews had been slain and that he had

> cables for some months, telling of these things. I succeeded, together with the heads of other Jewish organizations, in keeping these out of the press and have been in constant communications with the State Department, particularly Under Secretary Welles.(15)

On January 21, 1943, Leland Harrison - the American Minister to Switzerland - reported that

> Mass executions Poland now confirmed by different sources, one report states 6,000 killed daily one place Poland. Before being killed Jews must strip clothes being sent Germany. Remnants Jews Poland now confined 55 ghettos partly old ghettos larger towns partly small places transformed into ghettos. Certain number of Polish and deported Jews in labor camps in Poland and Silesia.
>
> Special Gestapo agents from Vienna where deportations were nearly completed, were sent to Berlin and Holland to speed up deportations. Even girls working in Berlin war industries whose parents already deported weeks before were suddenly arrested and deported. Sometimes children deported while parents at work. Many cases suicide about 2,000 hiding. Arrested people awaiting deportations in building without beds furniture.(16)

In early March 1943, Rabbi Wise pleaded with President Roosevelt that unless Hitler were stopped, there would be no Jews left in Europe.

> I beg you, dear President, as the recognized leader of the forces of democracy and humanity, to initiate action, which, if it cannot end the greatest crime ever perpetrated against a people, may yet save that people from utter extinction by offering asylum to its remnants in Sanctuaries to be created under the aegis of the U.N.(17)

The Jewish National Committee in Poland continued to ask Rabbi Wise, Nahum Goldmann and the J.D.C. for help:

March 17, 1943

This is to report to you the most dreadful crime of all times - the mass murder of millions of Jews in Poland. In the face of the acute danger that the still surviving Jews will be exterminated we appeal to you:

1. For vengeance on the Germans.
2. To force the Hitlerites to cease their murder.
3. To fight for our life and our honor.
4. For contact with neutral countries.
5. To save 10,000 of our children by means of exchange.

The remnants of Jewish communities in Poland exist in the conviction that during these most troubled days of our history you have not brought us help. Respond at least now in the last days of our life. This is our final appeal to you.(18)

President Roosevelt responded to the appeals of such men as Rabbi Stephen Wise by claiming that his Administration had "moved and continued to move, so far as the burden of war permits, to help the victims of the Nazis...."(19)

That was his response on March 23, 1943. In February, the U.S. Minsiter to Switzerland had been instructed via cable #354, signed by Sumner Wells, not to transmit any further reports from Gerhard Riegner on the atrocities. They seemed too hot to handle.

It is suggested that in the future reports submitted to you for transmission to private persons in the United States not be accepted unless extraordinary circumstances make such action advisable. It is felt that by sending such private messages which circumvent neutral countries' censorship we risk the possibilities that neutral countries might find it necessary to take step to curtail or abolish our official secret means of communication.(20)

But soon thereafter, on April 10, 1943, Welles sent Harrison another cable, this time asking him to transmit further information on the German barbarities. In his response, Harrison advised Welles that such reports should never have been suppressed in the first place. Had Secretary Welles' signature been forged? Was he oblivious to its meaning, or had he signed #354 with full knowledge of its content and later received countermanding orders from his superiors? Cable #354 remains a tragic mystery, but we do have the following account from Assistant Secretary Clement Dunn, dated December 22, 1944:

Dunn to Congressman Sol Bloom:

> I appreciate very much indeed your calling my attention today over the telephone to the statements made in the Senate the other day and carried in the *Congressional Record* for the proceedings of December 19, to the effect that I had obstructed or delayed telegrams being sent to our diplomatic missions abroad, with a view to bringing about help and assistance to certain Jewish persons or groups who are being held in German occupied countries.
>
> As I stated to you over the telephone and as I wish to make clear on the record, any allegations of this kind are false and without any foundation whatever.
>
> There was also reference in the *Congressional Record* of that date to my having been responsible for sending out a telegram to Berne, Switzerland, evidently at an earlier period, asking that mission to stop sending "atrocity stories." This allegation is entirely untrue. There was a telegram sent early in 1943 to Berne cautioning the American Legation against the use of our official and secret code facilities for the transmission of private cable messages for delivery to persons other than Government officials since such action might compromise this Government's secret channels of communications. That telegram was signed by Mr. Welles for the Secretary of State.(21)

## The Bermuda Conference

The atrocity reports helped embarass the Allies into taking what appeared to be more positive action. They could not very well claim that they were fighting for human decency and liberty if they refused to help the persecuted. This atempt to dispel the impression of callous indifference to human suffering manifested itself in another sham conference. This time the meeting took place on the island of Bermuda Ostensibly called to help the refugees, like so many previous meetings, the Anglo-American Bermuda Conference of April 1943, turned out to be a conference of words without action. When the United States and Great Britain excluded from the agenda any discussion of rescue operations in occupied Europe, reprisals against Germany, or Palestine as a place of refuge, they turned the conference into a travesty and burlesque.

Chaim Weizmann, President of the Jewish Agency for Palestine submitted the following memorandum asking that the conference consider Palestine as a place of refuge:

In the light of the overwhelming tragedy which faces the more than four million Jews which, it is estimated, still survive in the Nazi occupied countries, it is hoped that the governments of Great Britain, the United States and other members of the United Nations, would be ready to undertake practical steps commensurate with the vastness of the problem. Unhappily the statements of the Secretary of State for Foreign Affairs, Mr. Anthony Eden, and the United States Secretary of State Mr. Cordell Hull, give little support for this hope. The terms of reference for the Bermuda Conference are severely limited in scope and are intended apparently to deal only with the fringe of the problem rather than with the problem itself. While the Jewish Agency for Palestine is grateful for any measures which may be calculated to save the lives of at least some of Europe's Jews, it would be failing in its most elementary duty were it not to call attention to a situation which, overriding all ordinary political considerations, calls for a plan conceived on the broadest possible lines for the rescue of these four million Jews who are in imminent danger of physical annihilation.

...it must be borne in mind that of all peoples, the Jews have been singled out for utter and complete destruction by the enemy. Should the announced policy of the enemy continue unchecked, it is not impossible that by the time the war will have been won. the largest part of the Jewish population of Europe will have been exterminated. In these circumstances it is inconceivable that the democracies, engaged as they are in a struggle for world liberation, should fail to take fullest cognizance of the plight in which the Jews in Nazi occupied countries find themselves.

The statement that the world is divided into countries in which the Jews cannot live and countries which they must not enter has proven only too true. So far as Palestine is concerned, however, despite great obstacles, in spite too of the outbreak of war, the closing of the Mediterranean, there has been continued and rapid development, and a further substantial immigration has been absorbed. The Jewish population which numbered about 65,000 at the end of the last war has grown to about 550,000 today, and in the years since the rise of Hitler, Palestine has absorbed more immigration from Germany and German occupied Europe than any other country. It is to urge that both as an ad hoc reception center to which Jewish refugees may be brought and for the time being kept and maintained, and also as a place where in the long run the refugees may be absorbed into the general economy, Palestine should for the following reasons be given principal consideration:

A. As Jews coming to the Jewish National Home they would be welcomed in every possible way by their fellow Jews there. The spirit which animates the Jewish community of Palestine in this regard was given expression in a recent manifesto in the course of which it was stated that "the Jews of Palestine solemnly declare their willingness and readiness to extend shelter to all Jews who are leaving or who have left occupied territories, to share their bread, to save their brothers and sisters, fathers and mothers, from being led like sheep to the slaughter house."

B. From the practical point of view, Palestine by reason of its proximity to the Balkan countries has important geographical advantages. Transportation there from South Eastern Europe would be possible overland or by a relatively short sea-route....

C. Once in Palestine the gradual absorption and integration of these refugees into the economic life of the country could in due course be effected. It is estimated that for 50,000 there would be immediate possibilities of absorption within the framework of the present economic structure. The very great expansion of Palestine's agriculture and industry since the outbreak of the war, and the fact that 30,000 Palestine Jews are today serving in the armed forces of the U.N. has produced an acute shortage of labor which is in no degree met by current immigration.(22)

Weizmann believed that the Jews who had been deprived of their rights by the Nazi invaders and their collaborators would not want to return to their place of origins at the end of the war. He appealed to the conscience of the leaders of the democratic nations to assit the Jewish people in their time of great suffering. They could make no greater contribution than to help the homeless return to Erez Israel.

While the Jews were the main targets of the Nazis, the conference skirted around the Jewish question by insisting that ways be found to aid the persecuted of all faiths and races. The Allies seemed afraid of the word **Jew**. By British standards, if the Jewish problem were singled out, anti-Semitism would be aroused

## 42 Speak Not for the Jews Are Burning

"in areas where an excessive number of foreign Jews are introduced." While the conference exposed Britain's obsessive apprehension that Germany might change its policy from "extermination to one of extrusion," and thereby "flood" the world, and the British Empire in particular, with Jewish refugees, it also revealed that American quotas would remain most restrictive. Apparently live and homeless Jews were more embarassing to the Allies than dead ones. A letter of instruction to the American delegation reminded the delegates that

> care should be exercised to avoid placing the Government of the United States in a position where it could be accused of an attempt to fill with European refugees the places of our men and women in the armed services of the United States who have been sent to Europe to lay down their lives, if necessary, for the common cause.(23)

From the very start of the conference, both parties were so sure that it would fail that neither wanted it held in its territory. When British Bermuda was finally selected, Breckinridge Long noted that Anthony Eden had tried to place "responsibility and embarassment in our laps, now they have the baby again."(24) Both were responsible for failure at Bermuda. All they accomplished was to revive the inept, do-nothing Intergovernmental Committee and devise a limited plan whereby a few thousand Jews would be transported to greater safety from Spain to North Africa, and from Bulgaria to Palestine via Turkey. Those were the total results. The two Allies refused to negotiate with the Nazis on the grounds that such discussions could only serve the enemy. No attempt was made to encourage changing the existing immigration restrictions and there was no mention of rescuing those still in Nazi hands. They argued that the only way to rescue Jews was to win the war, and there was no sense in making rescue plans since Germany would never permit the Jews to leave. The 1944-1945 rescue of some Jews from the Balkans proved how wrong the Bermuda conferees had been.

Even the meagre gesture of transporting a few thousand people to the greater safety of North Africa and Palestine met with opposition. Admiral William D. Leahy found the proposed project unacceptable because he felt it would require the use of ships needed for the war effort, and place "unwarranted administrative responsibility on the Supreme Commander in North Africa" because the Arabs would be opposed to the introduction of Jews to North Africa.(25)

Leahy's arguments were fallacious. Allied vessels were not needed since the Jewish Agency had arranged to hire Italy's *Vulcania, Saturnia* and *Guilio Ceasare* for $5,000 a day. North Africa had many camps filled with prisoners of war, a few thousand Jews would have hardly caused "unwarranted administrative responsibility," and Arab opposition was more of a problem created in the mind of Admiral Leahy than in the Arab communities since Jews and Arabs had lived together in North Africa for centuries. As Churchill put it in a letter to Roosevelt:

> Our immediate facilities for helping victims of Hitler's anti-Jewish drive are so limited at present time that the opening of the small camp proposed for the purpose of removing some of them to safety seems all the more incumbant on us....Let's get this going.(26)

The Bermuda conference accomplished nothing, but that was no surprise to such individuals as Breckinridge Long:

> The truth of the whole thing is that there is no authority in this government that can make commitments to take refugees in groups and there are no funds out of which the expense of refugees could be paid for safe keeping in other localities and the immigration laws can't be changed.(27)

But those of Long's persuasion always insisted that there was nothing that could be done. They approached the problem from a defeatist viewpoint and they defeated every positive plan. They contended that there was no help that could be given the Jews short of military destruction of Germany's power. They felt that it was "improbable that Germany would permit the departure of Jews even if we could bring ourselves to the point of negotiating with the enemy during the course of the conflict."(28)

At Bermuda, the U.S. and Britain had not worked to rescue the persecuted, but to rescue themselves from public condemnation for a policy of callous indifference. Each was jealous of the other's pretended righteousness. Sumner Welles was disturbed by Britain's attempt to create the impression that it was "the great outstanding champion of the Jewish people and the sole defender of the rights of freedom of religion and individual liberty and that it was being held back...by the unwillingness of this Government to take any action for the relief of these unfortunates beyond words and gestures."(29) But the U.S. and Britain even failed to rescue themselves from public condemnation. No excuses revolving around the primacy of the war effort could undo the charge of fraud.

Secretary of State Hull advised the President in May 1943, not to let the refugees into America without first complying with the immigration laws and he did not favor a relaxation of those laws because he felt that such a move would only raise "prolonged and bitter controversy in Congress...." since Congress was anxious to make it even more difficult for outsiders to enter the U.S. Secretary of State Hull was opposed to the admission of refugees even on a temporary basis because he feared that Congress would then accuse Roosevelt of trying to evade existing laws. The President agreed: "I suggest that we do not give unlimited promises but that we undertake with Britain to share the cost of financing from time to time any specific cases."

Roosevelt would not do "other than comply strictly" with existing immigration laws. He opposed resurrecting the question of immigration laws as well as bringing in any more visitors on a temporary basis since "we have already brought in a large number."(30)

But in November 1943, Edward Stettinius would inform Mr. Long that the President felt not enough was being done for the Jewish refugees:

> He felt it might be possible to have a small office in Algiers, Naples, Portugal, Madrid, and Ankara with an American official in each to assist the Jews. He felt there might be a refugee camp such as the one in North Africa, and that a small amount of money might be made available for this purpose.(31)

**The War Refugee Board**

In a report to the President on January 16, 1944, Secretary of the Treasury Henry J. Morgenthau, Jr., reviewed the history of the diplomacy of rescue charging the Roosevelt Administration with having failed to "prevent the extermination of Jews in German controlled Europe; with procrastination in the rescue of the persecuted, deception and with outright censorship of atrocity reports;" and he advised the President that "only a fervent will to accomplish, backed by persistent and untiring

## Speak Not for the Jews Are Burning 45

effort, can succeed where time is so precious...." Unless the U.S. took some strong action, it would be "placed in the same position as Hitler and share the responsibility for exterminating all the Jews of Europe."(32) The abortive Bermuda conference and the atrocity reports apparently moved some Americans to urge their President to participate directly in saving the remnant of European Jewry. The same U.S. Congress that had opposed the relaxation of immigration quotas now pressured the President to create a special agency to help rescue Jews.

In his testimony before the House Foreign Affairs Committee in December 1943, Assistant Secretary Long painted an altogether false picture by asserting that America had done all it could to admit the refugees and that the doors had always been open. He presented 580,000 as the number of refugees admitted in the ten year period since the Nazis had begun their persecutions. But only 568,000 had been authorized and of those only 545,000 were issued, and very few Jews ever had a chance to use them thanks to the regulations strictly enforced by American consuls in Europe.

After testifying, Mr. Long got worried and he asked his State Department division to justify his misrepresentations: "They ask the question where we got the 580,000. We ought to be able to answer that."(33) Later he explained to Congressman Sol Bloom that he had made a small error in wording, instead of "We have taken into this country since the beginning of the Hitler regime... approximately 580,000 refugees" he felt that he should have said that only such a number of visas had been authorized. But Long still claimed that the Roosevelt Administration had "tried to be helpful to a large number of people and that we gave them an opportunity to escape from their oppressors and come to the United States."(34) He persisted in his distortion. From what Long claimed we should surmise that the Jews wanted to stay in Europe to be killed by German Nazis and their henchmen! What garbage! In his diary, Long would write that during "a long four hour Foreign Affairs Committee inquisition" he had made

> several statements which were not accurate - for I spoke without notes, from a memory of four years, without preparation and on one day's notice. It is remarkable I did not make more inaccurate statements. But the radical press, always prone to attack me, and the Jewish press have turned their barrage

against me and made life somewhat uncomfortable. I said "We have taken into this country approximately 580,000 refugees" (in ten years) and I should have said "We have authorized visas to come to this country." The figures are 568,000 authorized of which 545,000 issued. On that basis I have been pilloried as an enemy of the Jews and as trying to discredit them. Anyhow....their agitation depends on attacking some individual. So for the time being I am the bull's eye.(35)

Ira Hirschmann, the man who later claimed to have bypassed F.D.R.'s Breckinridge Long faction, and the man who would be credited by Arthur Morse for helping to rescue Jews from the Balkans,(36) seemed impressed by Long's performance as can be seen in the following letter he sent to Long on December 27, 1943:

I had occasion on Friday to lunch with Mr. Sulzberger....I handed him a full copy of your statement. He said he had already seen it, but not read it through, and I told him that I felt it was worth spending the time to do so fully. He said he would as he was deeply interested. I intend to bring it directly to the attention of other individuals who can disseminate the message.(37)

Was Long merely guilty of a minor error in wording? One wonders about the nature of such "little errors" especially after reading his confession to Avra Warren that the figures used before the Foreign Affairs Committee were the same he had used all along in briefing sessions with Roosevelt.(38)

On February 2, 1944, Robert Alexander of the State Department prepared the following text on the refugee issue for Long:

By taking the unused portion of the British quotas for the entire decade, which amounts to approximately 620,000 numbers, Mr. Celler (39) would try to show that 620,000 Jewish refugees were kept out of the U.S. because of the alleged unwillingness of the Department of State to fill all the quotas of the world. He would also apply the same formula to the other quotas of different countries of the world. Such an argument is based either upon ignorance of the law or is a deliberate attempt to mislead the public. In view of Mr. Celler's authorship and sponsorship of certain bills in Congress which, if they had been passed, would have taken the unused quotas into a special "jackpot for the Jews," Mr. Celler's pleas do not appear to be based upon ignorance of the law.(40)

On December 20, 1943, a resolution calling for the creation of a special rescue agency was unanimously endorsed by the Senate Foreign Relations Committee, but it got nowhere in the House Foreign Affairs Committee, which was presided over by Congressman Sol Bloom, a Jew who had been on the American delegation to the Bermuda conference. The hearings were discontinued on December 26, and no action was taken on the resolution.

President Roosevelt agreed to create a special agency only after Morgenthau threatened to publicize his report on how the U.S. failed to prevent the extermination of European Jewry and how the State Department suppressed the facts for fear of arousing American public opinion.

On January 22, 1944, Roosevelt announced the creation of a new interdepartmental commission to be known as the War Refugee Board, and composed of the Secretary of the Treasury Henry J. Morgenthau, Jr., Secretary of War Henry L. Stimson, and Under Secretary of State Edward R. Stettinius. It was commissioned to develop programs for the rescue, transportation, maintenance and relief of victims of enemy oppression. Stressing the need to frustrate Nazi extermination plans, Roosevelt declared that the W.R.B. would seek the cooperation of all friendly and neutral states and international bodies to rescue the persecuted.

The W.R.B. made some progress. It even obtained greater cooperation from the Vatican. When in October 1942, the "free world" declared itself against German atrocities, President Roosevelt had asked Pope Pius XII to likewise denounce the Nazis, but Pius refused. The Pope rejected the atrocity reports as greatly exaggerated for "propaganda" purposes and he maintained that his previous statements denouncing murder committed for no reason other than nationality or race was sufficient. Moreover, he insisted that he could not denounce the Nazis without also attacking the horrors committed by the Bolsheviks, and he believed that such declarations would hardly be pleasing to the Allies.(41)

## 48  Speak Not for the Jews Are Burning

> Mr. Harold H. Tittmann, Assistant to the President's Personal Representative to Pope Pius XII, to the Secretary of State
>
> Vatican City, October 6, 1942.
>
> The Holy See is still apparently convinced that a forthright denunciation by the Pope of Nazi atrocities, at least in so far as Poland is concerned, would only result in the violent deaths of many more people. Mgr. Montini, however, stated to me that the time may come when, in spite of such a grievous prospect, the Holy Father will feel himself obliged to speak out.
>
> In addition to the reasons enumerated in my despatch no 109 of September 8, 1942, another motive, possibly the controlling one, behind the Pope's disinclination to denounce Nazi atrocities is his fear that if he does so now, the German people, in the bitterness of their defeat, will reproach him later on for having contributed, if only indirectly, to this defeat. It has been pointed out to me that just such an accusation was directed against the Holy See by the Germans after the last war, because of certain phrases spoken and attitudes adopted by Benedict XV while hostilities were in progress. When it is borne in mind that Pius XII had many years of conditioning in Germany, it will not seem unnatural that he should be particularly sensible to this particular argument.
>
> Respectfully yours,
> Harold H. Tittmann

In February 1943, mass deportations of Jews from Italy took place, but even then Pius and his Secretary of State (the present day Pope Paul) refused to protest. Some observers excused the Pope's unwillingness to act on the grounds that the Church would have been endangered, but others felt that Pius was quite secure in view of the "consideration with which Germans have so far treated the Holy See."(42) The Pope had failed to speak out when his word was so badly needed, but when his own personal safety and position was threatened, he found it appropriate to raise his voice in protest. Even then he spoke out against the Allies and not the Nazis. Said Pope Pius:

> Slaughter and destruction can contribute very little to world peace.
>
> The destruction and damaging of churches, charitable institutions, and artistic monuments, even when this destruction is not needed...are doing much harm to the Allied cause. They are actually diminishing the prestige of the United States....

## Speak Not for the Jews Are Burning 49

Pius warned that such Allied bombings would result in the triumph of communism and he asked President Roosevelt to spare Italy from needless vengeance.(43)

American observers found Pius' words of recrimination rather strange. Where had the Pope been during the past twenty years when Italy committed aggression and made war. American diplomatic observers found it hard to appreciate the Pope's concern for a few monuments in Rome.(44) They also wondered where he had been when other civilizations were being brutalized by the Nazis. Why hadn't he spoken out when the Germans and their allies set out to destroy millions of innocent people and their countries? They wondered if the Pope's concern for Rome was genuine. Perhaps he was more concerned with the preservation of his own position and power, because if Rome were bombed, then the world might conclude that somehow the great Pope Pius of Rome did not have much influence, after all, that he was not the "father" of all mankind.(45) As Roosevelt wrote to Pius XII on July 19, 1943:

> His Holiness again expressed his concern over the fate of the Italian people. Unfortunately, the government of Italy for a period of twenty years has glorified the use of force and has used it ruthlessly against the Greeks, the Ethiopians, the Albanians - to mention only a few of the victims of the Fascist aggression. The people of Italy have been made the instrument of this pagan policy. When the Italians are liberated from Fascist domination and are free once more to demonstrate their innate good judgment, they will be given an opportunity to choose the kind of government based on democratic principles that they may wish to establish. It is my intention...that Italy will be restored to nationhood after the defeat of Fascism and will take her place as a respected member of the European family of nations.(46)

The Pope's response of July 20 was typical of many such correspondences which fill volume 7 of the Vatican's 1942 documents:

> It is a prayer that everywhere, as far as humanly possible, the civil population be spared the horrors of war; that the homes of God's poor be not laid in ashes; that the little ones and youth, a nation's hope, be preserved from all harm - how Our heart bleeds when We hear of helpless children made victims of cruel war - ; that churches dedicated to the worship of God and monuments that enshrine the memory and masterpieces of human genius be protected from destruction. We repeat this appeal

unwilling to yield to any thought of its hopelessness, although almost daily We must continue to deplore the evils against which We pray. And now even in Rome, parent of western civilization and for well nigh two thousand years centre of the Catholic world, to which millions, one may risk the assertion, hundreds of millions of men throughout the world have recently been turning their anxious gaze. We have had to witness the harrowing scene of death leaping from the skies and stalking pitilessly through unsuspecting homes striking down women and children; and in person We have visited and with sorrow contemplated the gaping ruins of that ancient and priceless Papal basilica of St. Laurence, one of the most treasured and loved sanctuaries of all Supreme Pontiffs, and visited with devotion by pilgrims from all countries of the world.

But since Divine Providence has placed Us head over the Catholic Church and Bishop of this city so rich in sacred shrines and hallowed, immortal memories, We feel it Our Duty to voice a particular prayer and hope that all may recognize that a city, whose every district, in some districts every street has its irreplaceable monuments of faith or art and Christian culture, cannot be attacked without inflicting an incomparable loss on the patrimony of Religion and Civilization.(47)

In February 1944, the War Refugee Board asked for Papal intervention to help save 15,000 Jews about to be deported from Slovakia. Secretary Stettinius asked the Pope to warn Dr. Tiso, Catholic ruler of Slovakia, of future punishment on earth and damnation in hell if he would continue to persecute the Jews. This time the Vatican did intervene, but Tiso's reply was that the Jews were not being exterminated, just temporarily interned. Cardinal Cicognani, the Papal representative in Washington, assured the State Department that "the Holy See will continue its interest in the welfare of those unfortunate people."(48)

As the W.R.B. was not satisfied with Tiso's response, it continued to press for further assurances that Jews would not be transported to Germany and late in May, Tiso asserted that he had "no intention" of deporting Jews; but Church officials warned that he could not be trusted. They were right, for the Jews of Slovakia were almost totally annihilated.(49)

When the W.R.B. intervened at the Vatican on behalf of the Hungarian Jews, Secretary of State Hull asked Pope Pius to warn

## Speak Not for the Jews Are Burning 51

Hungarian Christians of the spiritual consequences to the perpetrators of atrocities:

> we earnestly suggest that His Holiness may find it appropriate to express himself on this subject to the authorities and people of Hungary personally by radio and through the Nuncio and clergy in Hungary as well as through a representative of the Holy See especially dispatched to Hungary for that purpose.(50)

In effect, the Pope was asked to help save the remaining 800,000 Jews of Hungary and a month after this appeal, Pope Pius telegraphed Admiral Horthy asking him that everything possible be done in Hungary to help "the many unfortunate persons who are suffering because of their race or nationality." Pius did not use the word Jews, but his appeal did help convince Horthy that he should not permit the atrocities to continue.(51)

It should be noted that while Pius may have been reluctant to help the Jews, there were other churchmen like Angelo Roncalli, the Vatican's Apostolic Delegate to Turkey, who did help. Roncalli intervened with the King of Bulgaria to help the Jews of Bulgaria. He provided baptismal certificates to save thousands of Jews, and he obtained Palestine immigration papers from the British for a number of Jews.(52)

After much urging from Henry Morgenthau, Jr., Edward Stettinius and Henry Stimson, the President finally issued a strongly worded warning to those committing atrocities. This declaration of March 1944, in which the Jews were specifically mentioned as the people being persecuted, referred to the Nazi atrocities as the blackest crimes of all time, and warned that "none who participate in these acts of savagery shall go unpunished. All who share the guilt shall share the punishment." It would be "a major tragedy" said the declaration, that the innocents who had survived more than ten years of "Hitler's fury should perish on the very eve of the triumph over the barbarians." All friendly and neutral states were asked to open their doors to the immigrants, and the U.S. offered to pay all expenses.(53)

> In one of the blackest crimes of all history - begun by the Nazis in the day of peace and multiplied by them a hundred times in time of war - the wholesale systematic murder of the Jews of Europe goes on unabated every hour. As a result of the events of the last few days, hundreds of thousands of Jews who while

## 54 Speak Not for the Jews Are Burning

1   Bund Archives, New York City.
2   Nahum Goldmann, *The Autobiography of Nahum Goldmann, Sixty Years of Jewish Life* (New York, 1969) 147-148.
3   Justin Wise Polier and James Waterman Wise, ed., *The Personal Letters of Stephen S. Wise* (Boston, 1956) 232-234, 260-261.
4   *Summary of Proceedings of War Emergency Conference of World Jewish Congress,* November 24-30, 1944, World Jewish Congress Archives, New York City.
5   Interview with Gerhard Riegner, April 20, 1973.
6   *Ibid.*
7   *Ibid.*
8   *Ibid.*
9   *Ibid.*
10  *Ibid.*
11  World Jewish Congress Archives.
12  John Morton Blum, *From the Morgenthau Diaries, Years of War, 1941-1945* (Boston, 1967) 207-227. Hereafter cited as Blum, *Years of War.* Interview with G. Riegner, April 20, 1973.
13  *Ibid.*
14  Ben Hecht to F.D.R., Telegram, November 4, 1943, State Department File No. 840.48 Refugees/4854, National Archives, Washington, D.C.
15  Stephen S. Wise to F.D.R., December 2, 1942, Stephen S. Wise Papers, Brandeis University.
16  Leland Harrison to Under Secretary of State, Telegram, January 21, 1943, State Department File No. 740.00116 European War 1939/ 753, National Archives, Washington, D.C.
17  Stephen S. Wise to F.D.R., March 4, 1943, Stephen S. Wise Papers, Brandeis University.
18  Jewish National Committee in Poland to Rabbi Wise, Nahum Goldmann and the J.D.C., March 17, 1943, J.D.C. Papers, New York City.
19  F.D.R. to Stephen S. Wise, March 23, 1943, Stephen S. Wise Papers, Brandeis University.
20  Cordell Hull and Sumner Wells to Leland Harrison, Telegram February 10, 1943, State Department File No. 740.00116 E.W. 1939/753 PSMW, National Archives, Washington, D.C.
21  Assistant Secretary Clement Dunn to Congressman Sol Bloom, December 22, 1944, State Department File No. 740.00116 E.W. 1939/753 PSMW, National Archives, Washington, D.C.
22  Weizmann Memorandum, April 1943, Jewish Agency Papers, Zionist Archives, New York City.
23  *Foreign Relations of the United States,* January 20, 1943, I, 134-137.

24  Breckinridge Long Diary, March 19, 1943, Library of Congress.
25  *Foreign Relations of the United States,* April 26, 1943, I, 296-297.
26  *Ibid.,* June 30, 1943, I, 321.
27  Breckinridge Long Diary, June 23, 1943, Library of Congress.
28  *Foreign Relations of the United States,* June 29, 1943, I, 319-321.
29  *Ibid.,* March 6, 1943, I, 145.
30  *Ibid.,* May 14, 1943, I, 179.
31  Edward R. Stettinius to B. Long, November 11, 1943, State Department File No. 867N.01/2042, National Archives, Washington, D.C.
32  Blum, *Years of War,* 207-227. *F.D.R. and Morgenthau* (Boston, 1970), 532-533.
33  Long to Travers, December 16, 1943, Breckinridge Long Papers, Library of Congress.
34  Long to Sol Bloom, December 31, 1943, Breckinridge Long Papers, Library of Congress.
35  B. Long Diary, January 1, 1944, The Library of Congress.
36  See Ira Hirschmann's *Life to a Promised Land. Caution to the Winds* and *Red Star Over Bethlehem.* Of interest also is Arthur Morse's *While Six Million Died* (New York, 1967), Hereafter cited as Morse, *Six Million.*
37  Ira Hirschmann to Breckinridge Long, December 27, 1943, State Department File No. 840.48 Refugees/4009, National Archives, Washington, D.C.
38  Long to A. Warren, January 7, 1944, Breckinridge Long Papers.
39  Congressman Emanuel Celler of Brooklyn, New York.
40  Memo prepared by R. Alexander for B. Long, February 2, 1944, Breckinridge Long Papers, Library of Congress.
41  *Foreign Relations of the United States,* January 5, 1943, II, 911-913.
42  *Ibid.,* October 29, 1943 II, 951.
43  *Ibid.,* August 20, 1943, II 945-946.
44  *Actes et Documents du Saint Siege Relatives a la Seconde Guerre Mondiale* (Vatican, 1973) vol. VII, 136-138, 179-180. Hereafter cited as *Actes et Documents du S. Siege.*
45  *Foreign Relations of the United States,* July 10, 19, 28, 31, 1943, II, 930-939.
46  *Ibid.*
47  *History of the War Refugee Board with Selected Documents,* January 22, 1944 - September 15, 1945, February 21, 26, 1944, 1128-9. Hereafter cited as *W.R.B.*
49 *W.R.B.* April 3; May 24; October 14; November 14; December 1, 1944, 1130-1139.
50  *W.R.B.,* May 26, 1944, 1142-1143.

51 *W.R.B.* July 7, 24, 1944, 1144-1146.
52 Morse, *Six Million*, 320-322, 365, 366, 369.
53 *Foreign Relations of the United States,* August 27, 1943, II, 416.
54 *Ibid.*
55 Visa Division Memorandum to Mr. Alexander, November 20, 1943, State Department File No. FW 840.48 Refugees/4854, National Archives, Washington, D.C.
56 Chaim Weizmann to Field Marshall Smuts, August 15, 1941, Robert Szold Papers, Zionist Archives, New York.

# CHAPTER IV

## Failures to Rescue

Roosevelt may have finally issued declarations, he may have asked others to join in protest, he may have asked neutrals like Portugal, Turkey, Spain, Sweden, Switzerland, the Latin American states, and the British Commonwealth to admit Jews, he may have created the War Refugee Board to help rescue Jews, and he may have offered to provide funds for the upkeep of the refugees; but he still refused to open up America to them

Throughout the war years there were numerous chances to save Jews via negotiations with the Nazis, but the U.S. and Britain refused to take advantage of those chances, claiming that such discussions would only damage Allied unity and that the Germans were insincere.

Greatly concerned with relocating Jews and afraid that they might seek Palestine as their homeland and thereby upset Britain's Arab Empire, the British refused to even consider such discussions with the Germans. They preferred - so they said - to throw the matter into the laps of the Intergovernmental Committee on Refugees, an organization proven by its inaction to be a dead end agency. But in fact they preferred to see them dead. In September 1943, the British had proclaimed that all Jews escaping Nazi dominated territories and entering Turkey would be permitted to enter Palestine after a security check. But by August 1944, when some Jews had managed to escape, the British reneged and claimed that there was no room for the refugees in Palestine. Thanks to the support they received from President Roosevelt, the British did not even permit the 100,000 Jews into Palestine as they had promised in their 1939 White Paper.

58   Failures to Rescue

**Ransom and Slovakia**

One of the lost opportunities involved Slovakia's Jews. The plan to rescue Slovakia's Jews through ransom was conceived by Gisi Fleischmann, a Zionist. She had smuggled children out of Poland and later out of Slovakia with the help of J.D.C. funds. As these limited operations had worked, she thought of asking Dieter Wisliceny, assistant to Adolf Eichmann, how much it would take to stop the deportations from Slovakia. His answer was 50,000 Pounds Sterling. While the Jews would have to live in labor camps, they would not be deported. Gisi asked for time in which to contact the interested Jewish organizations. She was given one month's time. Gisi turned to Saly Mayer, J.D.C. representative in Switzerland, but he was reluctant to turn over such a sum of money to the Nazis. Moreover, he informed Gisi that he would need the approval of the U.S. before he could release the funds.(1)

Wisliceny ordered the deportations to stop and awaited his 50,000 Pounds. Gisi finally obtained the money from the Jewish Agency office in Constantinople. Unfortunately, the money arrived after the stated deadline, and to show that he meant business, Wisliceny sent some 3,000 Jews to their death from September 18 to October 20, 1942; but from that date until October 1944, when the Slovakians revolted against the Nazis, not one transport of Jews was sent out of Slovakia.

Then came the **Europa plan.** It was the Nazi Wisliceny, with approval from Himmler, who informed Gisi that if she would provide $2 million, the deportations would be stopped everywhere in Europe except Germany and Poland. With $2 million, she could save the lives of over one million Jews. Two dollars a Jew. The Jewish Agency made known its readiness to accept the offer, and the Yishuv prepared to send $100,000. But when the J.D.C. was asked to furnish the rest, it refused, saying that it could not disperse such funds without U.S. approval. The J.D.C. claimed that it was prepared to place $2 million in escrow either in a U.S. or a Swiss bank in Wisliceny's name. Gisi got nowhere with the J.D.C., and after much travail obtained $57,000 from the Jewish Agency. She gave that sum to the Nazis as an advance payment and she asked for a further delay. They gave her two more weeks, but when that time elapsed, Wisliceny returned the $57,000, perhaps to show that he had meant business. Gisi had failed because the J.D.C. could not obtain U.S. clearance. Perhaps J.D.C. did not know it, but the U.S. awaited British clearance. Britain refused to give its approval. Foreign Minister Eden was concerned that the Nazis might release their Jewish captives. The J.D.C. lacked initiative to bypass such British-American rules and regulations.(2)

While Gisi had been negotiating with the Nazis, American and British officials met in Bermuda and refused to devise any feasible plan to help save the Jews; and Goebbels observed publicly that the very same countries that had expressed sympathy for the Jews were unwilling to receive them.

**Trucks for Jews**

Joel Brand, a member of the Council for Assistance and Rescue in Hungary, knew of the negotiations between Gisi and Wisliceny. He knew that one transaction had been successful, and he knew of the **Europa plan** "according to which Wisliceny would save all the Jews in Europe for two or three million dollars."(3) And Brand tried to establish contact with Wisliceny. According to his testimony at the Jerusalem trial of Adolf Eichmann, it cost the Hungarian Jews some $25,000 to establish contact with that Nazi and when they did, Brand asked four things from Wisliceny:
1. No concentration of Jews into ghettos.
2. No pogroms.
3. No deportations.
4. Permission for Jews to emigrate to Palestine.

He asked that the Jews be permitted to go to Palestine because until that time "there was a legal emigration of about 50 Jewish children a month to Palestine...." The Jews of Hungary were prepared to give Wisliceny $2 million in 10 monthly installments. Their "assumption was that the war would be over within ten months."(4)

Wisliceny agreed to three of the four demands made by Brand. He agreed not to force the Jews into the ghetto, that there would be no pogroms and no deportations, but he added that the S.S. could not be bodyguards: "When wood is being cut, chips must fall." As for emigration from Hungary, he would not agree to the exodus of only a few Jews, he wanted the entire Jewish population of Hungary to leave; but not to Palestine since the Mufti was against that. He demanded a downpayment of $200,000, and it was made in several installments.(5)

Towards April 25, 1944, contact was made with Eichmann. He was not interested in money. According to Brand's testimony, Eichmann returned some money. Said Eichmann to Brand: "You see, here there are about $50,000 to $57,000 and 72,000 francs. These came here within the framework of rescue for children. I have no objections to helping children. Here is the money and here are the letters. Most of them are written in Yiddish, Hebrew and Polish." Eichmann wanted 10,000 trucks and he would release one million Jews for them. "One hundred Jews for one truck and that's a pretty good price for you." He promised Brand that if he would return from his mission of talking with the Allied and Jewish representatives "with an affirmative reply, then he would blow up the Auschwitz installations and would be prepared to let us have ten percent of the one million Jews; that is, he would give us 100,000 Jews and place them at any border we name, and only then would we have to give him the first ten percent of the trucks, that is the first one thousand trucks."(6)

When Joel Brand reached Constantinople, he discovered Jewish leaders divided and Allied leaders unwilling to listen. The German offer of Jewish blood for goods became known to Secretary of State Hull a few days after Brand arrived in Constantinople. Lawrence Steinhardt, then the U.S. Ambassador to Turkey, reported that the Germans had promised to end the deportations and exterminations, and permit the Jews to leave if the Allies would provide Germany with 10,000 trucks, two million cakes of soap, 200 tons of cocoa, 800 tons of coffee and 200 tons of tea. Jews could depart from Hungary for such states as Spain in unlimited numbers, but only a limited number would be permitted to leave for Palestine, because the Germans, like their British counterparts, were afraid of arousing Arab opposition to their cause.(7)

After an agonizing month of trying to make direct contact in Ankara, Brand was informed that he would get his chance to meet Allied military officials in Aleppo, Syria. Disregarding a warning that the British were out to trap him and kill his mission, he went to Allepo. There he met British officials and Moshe

## Failures to Rescue 61

Shertok (Sharett) of the Jewish Agency and after telling his story, the British arrested him. No matter how much he pleaded that the Germans would view his detention as Allied unwillingness to trade, and that this would result in the mass murder of the remnant of European Jewry, his captors would not let him go. They were no more receptive to his supplications than they had been to the various pleas made on behalf of the refugees from 1933 to 1944.(8)

Sometimes Brand wondered if his mission was authentic. One such time was when Brandi Grosz, his companion, confided that the real purpose of the mission was for Grosz to initiate peace discussions with the Allies, and that the mission to save the Jews was just a front for Grosz' mission to make contact with the Allies and initiate peace discussions.(9)

After much travail, special emissary Ira Hirschmann discovered that Brand was being held in Egypt but, according to Hirschmann, Lord Moyne, Deputy Minister of State and senior British officer in the Middle East, refused to permit him to see Brand, and he referred him to Foreign Minister Eden. Hirschmann insisted that he had special orders from Washington to confer with Brand and that he intended to carry out his instructions. Hirschmann got to see Brand and promised him freedom, but Brand was to remain in jail for many months thereafter.(10)

On June 13, 1944, Burton Y. Berry, the American Consul General in Turkey, wrote the Secretary of State the following report on his views concerning the Brand mission:

> While the exact nature of Gyorgy's business in Turkey is a matter of some debate the purpose of Brand's trip is clear. His mission was to place certain German proposals before the representatives of Jewish relief and rescue organizations in Istanbul.
>
> These proposals, which Brand attributed to a source high in the German Gestapo, appear to be genuine in origin. Despite this fact, they were not taken seriously by most observers in Istanbul, but did receive a hearing from Jewish representatives in Turkey.
>
> ..."the Brand proposals," allegedly an official German proposal to free the Jews in occupied Europe in exchange for nominal

shipments of food supplies, soap and 10,000 trucks "to be used only on the Russian front."

Brand states that he came to Istanbul in an attempt to save the Jews of Hungary. He reports that all Jews in many sections of Hungary have been placed in concentration camps or ghettos, and that this procedure will be extended to other parts of the country as soon as possible. He adds that 12,000 Jews are being shipped to Poland for liquidation each day.

Brand's documentation as a Jewish emissary appears to be fairly satisfactory. It cannot be ascertained, however, whether his letters represent German manipulation or Jewish desire. It is possible that his communications are part of the German plot. It is more probable, of course, that the Jewish leaders in Hungary, aware of the peril of their situation, were willing to use the emissary provided by the Gestapo, and accordingly granted him appropriate documentation.

Two factors are of importance in determining the validity of this offer: 1. Does Brand take it seriously? 2. Do the German sponsors take it seriously?

As to the first question, Brand himself seems to hesitate in making a decision. He clearly indicated, in his last interview before leaving Istanbul, that he had little hope of actually getting many Jews out of Europe. He implied that he was playing his present role in the hope that by "playing for time" the Jews in Hungary might be assisted. He seemed to feel that, while the proposals will have no definite result, the time consumed in connection with them may postpone the liquidation of Jews in Hungary for a sufficient period to see the turn of the tide in Europe.

It seems probable that Brand himself has little faith in the success of his proposals, or in the German intention to keep their part of the bargain, even if the proposals were accepted by the Allies.

Conclusions

The proposals are a plot to place the Allies in a bad light, since they are designed for refusal, and will permit the German propagandists to say: "We offered to save the Jews, but the Allies turned us down!"

There would be an advantage in lightening the burden on the German conscience. There would be a possible advantage in preparing for the the peace table. The actual benefits, however, in war terms, would be minor. If we assume that the Germans are still placing their bets on, if not victory, at least a stalemate, then it is improbable that they would elaborate a propaganda campaign to prove a point of value only in case of defeat.

The proposals are part of an effort to split the Allies, divide Russia from Great Britain and the United States.

Comment:

If it is accepted that Germany can win a stalemate only by dividing the Allies, then it can be assumed that every effort will be made, up to the last minute to split Russia away from the Allied camp. Such an end can be achieved best, if it can be achieved at all, only by convincing the Russians that the Allies are not playing an open and honest game. How better could this be attained than by demonstrating that the Allies were considering a proposal that made military equipment available to the Germans for use against the Russians.

Whether this or some other conclusion is the logical "reason" for the Brand proposals, it can safely be assumed that the Istanbul trip of Brand and Gyorgy fit into some neat corner of the German master propaganda plan.(11)

Brand was not released even though the Allies urged a continuation of talks with the Nazis.(12) President Roosevelt instructed his diplomats to "keep talking." "Cable back everything you hear. While you talk, these people still have a chance to live." The Russians suspected that the talks were screens for separate Western peace negotiations with the Germans, and they were opposed to any deals.(13)

The negotiations continued, but so did the exterminations. Every passing day brought with it the death of tens of thousands of Jews. The War Refugee Board received reports of how the Hungarian regime cooperated with the bloodthirsty German Gestapo. Old people, men, women and children were herded into boxcars by military police who drove them on with rifle butts and whips. Young girls were turned over to the German soldiers and made into war harlots.(14)

The United States warned the Germans and their associates that they would be held responsible for their crimes and that the guilty would be punished. President Roosevelt's March 24, 1944 declaration was repeated: "None who participate in these acts of savagery shall go unpunished. All who share the guilt shall share the punishment."

Thus as we view the history of the Holocaust, we find that most of the states of the world refused to provide shelter to the Jews of Europe during the period of the Nazi reign of terror. There were very few exceptions and the refuge that such nations as Denmark, Sweden and Italy provided was limited, meagre and uncertain. Countries like the U.S.A., Britain, Australia, New Zealand and Brazil, that needed more people, especially active and industrious people, refused to provide even temporary shelter to the Jews. Moreover, they refused to issue declarations and warnings to stop the destruction of European Jewry. The callousness did not end there. Not only had they refused to issue declarations specifically referring to the murder of Jews, but they refused to help liberate the camps or bomb the railways or crematoriums. Some aspects of the Allied refusal to bomb the death camp facilities were revealed through Dr. Chaim Weizmann's story as documented during the Eichmann trial. But there's more to this story.

Some Jewish leaders like Dr. Weizmann believed that if the railways and camps were bombed, deportations and exterminations would be slowed down, if not stopped altogether. Others were opposed to bombings and called for Allied parachutists to liberate the camps. Jewish spokesmen were again divided and again failed to provide a united front before the non-Jews who wielded the power. Whatever the request, which Jewish leaders may have made, the answer was still no.

On June 27, 1944, Ignacy Schwarzbart, a General Zionist and a member of the Polish National Council in London, wrote to Stanislaw Mikoljczyk, the Prime Minister of the Polish-Government-in-Exile that since the Polish Army (the underground) was carrying out extensive actions against the Germans, the time was ripe to liberate the "victims imprisoned in diverse camps at Oswiecim, Majdanek, Treblinka...and many others." Schwarzbart suggested two means of doing this: "to bomb from the air the administrative buildings...and to arrange an armed attack on the camps by units of our Underground Army in order to rescue the victims." He said that he realized that both actions were fraught with danger and difficulties, and he therefore suggested that perhaps some "combined operation might achieve our purpose."

This rescue would be the only way "to prevent Hitler from continuing his actions of deporting people to Poland...." He concluded by advising the exiled Polish Prime Minister of some other ways of saving the Jews. The Polish Jews should be armed so that they could defend themselves. "The greatest possible number of Jews" should be permitted into the underground, and somehow the Jewish children should be saved.(15)

But on July 1, 1944, the head of the World Jewish Congress Rescue department, Leon Kubowitzki, wrote to John W. Pehle, head of the War Refugee Board, that he was opposed to bombing the camps. He urged that some other method be found to destroy "the gas chambers, the gas vans, the death baths" and in that way the "pace of the extermination" could be "considerably slowed down." He reminded Pehle that in August and October of 1943, Jews had successfully revolted and that they had destroyed the murder apparatus in a number of camps. Moreover, the revolt resulted in the escape of a large number of Jews from these camps. He categorically stated his opposition to bombing the camps from the air. And he underlined that view:

> The destruction of the death installations cannot be done by bombing from the air, as the first victims would be the Jews.(16)

Instead of bombing, Kubowitzki urged that the Russians be asked to dispatch paratroopers to seize the buildings, to annihilate the murderers and free the inmates, and the "Polish Government be requested to instruct the Polish underground to attack these and similar camps to destroy the instruments of death."(17)

John J. McCloy, Assistant Secretary of War, seemed to agree with him for he wrote to John Pehle that such bombings were "impracticable" since they would only take needed air support away from the military "engaged in decisive operations," and then such bombings would be "of such doubtful efficacy that it would not amount to a practical project."(18) The U.S. would not support the bombings.

Kubowitzki's intervention seems strange. Did not this Jewish leader know that the Russian army had refused to help the fighters of the Warsaw Rebellion in January - May 1943? Did he not know that the Polish Home Army, as the Polish underground was called, had, for the most part, refused to help Jewish fight-

## 66   Failures To Rescue

ers? Did he not know that some units of that underground even sought to kill Jews?

While the Kubowitzkis of the Jewish world were expressing their opposition to bombings, Dr. Chaim Weizmann went to see British Foreign Minister Anthony Eden to ask that the camps be bombed. On July 6, 1944, Weizmann went to see Foreign Minister Eden about the Brand deal and at the same time he asked that the Allies bomb the railways and crematoriums. Eden maintained that he neded American and Soviet approval on such matters as the Brand deal. Weizmann asked that in the interim, the Allies should publish a declaration that they were prepared to accept Jewish refugees in all their territories, and that neutral countries such as Sweden, Switzerland, perhaps Turkey, provide humanitarian shelter to refugees from the extermination camps. The Swiss Government, he urged, should be requested to inform the Hungarian authorities about its willingness to issue documents of immunity and passports in as great a number as possible for the Jewish refugees. And then he asked that the Allies should issue a warning that anyone who helped in the deportation of the Jews would be held responsible and punished, and that the railway lines leading to the extermination camps, and the extermination camps themselves should be bombed. On July 15, Mr. Randall of the Foreign Office informed Sharett that Weizmann's proposals to bomb the death camps and railways was under consideration. The answer came on September 1, 1944, from Permanent Under Secretary Richard Law:

> You will remember that in your meeting on the 6th of July, you spoke with the Foreign Secretary about the bombing of the Birkenau death camp, and about the atrocities which were committed there by the Germans toward Hungarian and other Jews.
>
> The matter was discussed to the fullest extent by a team of the Air Force, but I regret to inform you that because of the great technical difficulties involved, we have no choice but to refrain from using your proposal under the present circumstances. I understand that this decision will be a disappointment to you, but be sure that the matter was considered exhaustively.(19)

What were those technical difficulties of which Richard Law spoke? He could not have been referring to the bombing capacity of the Allies because by 1944, they held air supremacy throughout Europe. Allied planes had penetrated the entire region of eastern and central Europe. They dropped supplies to their troops and to partisans. They even managed to pick up their downed pilots, but they refused to drop weapons and equipment to the Jews in the ghettos or camps.(20)

The official U.S. reply to Kubowitzki's suggestions came from John J. McCloy on September 3, 1944. McCloy advised that operational troops could not be diverted to liberate the Jews. His reply was couched in Anglo-Saxon bureaucratese, but it was still a no. We will not save the Jews.

WAR DEPARTMENT
OFFICE OF THE ASSISTANT SECRETARY
WASHINGTON, D.C.

3 September 1944

Mr. A. Leon Kubowitzki
World Jewish Congress
1834 Broadway
New York 23, N.Y.

Dear Mr. Kubowitzki:
I have your letter of August 30, 1944.

The use of operational troops to which you refer in your letter must be subject to the discretion of the theater commander. Such operations as you suggest would fall within the jurisdiction of the Allied Mediterranean Commander, and he has been fully informed of the situation obtaining in the "death camp areas." He must be the judge of the practicality of such an operation and its likely results. I am sure he would do anything he felt he could to check these ghastly excesses of the Nazis. Perhaps an alteration in the tactical situation may make it possible for him to take some effective steps along the lines you propose.
Sincerely,
John J. McCloy (21)

Kubowitzki refused to give up. He went directly to the Russians as Dr. Nahum Goldmann had done a while back. Kubowitzki informed the Russians that reliable information pointed to German plans "to speed up the pace of the killings going on in the death factories of the camps they have set up in Poland." He reminded the Russians that Dr. Goldmann had asked the Russian Ambassador to the U.S. to convey this request to the Soviet authorities in Moscow, and since there was "alarmingly little time left" to save the "victims of German barbarism" Kubowitzki again made the request for Russian intervention on behalf of the people in the camps. He said that he realized that "the use of operational troops must be subject to the discretion of the Theater Commander" and he asked that the Commander be advised of the conditions in the camps. Thousands of inmates and millions of people throughout the world were hoping for "the speedy intervention of the Soviet paratroops." He concluded by asking the Russians to help save the 200,000 Jews of Budapest, Hungary. He asked that the Soviet Commander of the area warn the Germans and Hungarians "that inexorable retribution would be exacted from those who would lift their hands against the 200,000 ...." This time he asked for bombing of the railroads. He asked that the Russians bomb the railroad hubs of Budapest, Novy-Zamkey, Satoraljaujhely, Kosice, Estergom, Komaron and Gyor to "paralyze the deportation movements by railroad."(22)

The World Jewish Congress representative also went to see John J. McCloy on September 28, and he learned that the Allied Mediterranean Commander had been fully informed of the situation in the death camps. He advised the Jews to seek British assistance in this matter since the British were "in a better position to advise General Wilson on the steps which could be taken."(23)

Less than a week later, on October 4, 1944, Kubowitzki again contacted McCloy and asked for U.S. military intervention to help save the remnant of Jews in concentration camps. He told McCloy of German plans to kill off the remaining 50,000 prisoners in Oswiecim. The Germans were planning to use "artillery and bombers so that all proof of the crimes committed by the Germans be eliminated." The Jewish representative said that he was awaiting "most anxiously" to hear "about the steps taken by the War Department in this connection."(24) Kubowitzki and the rest of the Jews would have a long wait for the Allies still refused to help save the Jews. There were still "technical difficulties" and it was still "of doubtful efficacy" to help save the Jews.

While Nazis were wiping out European Jewry, and the Allies refused to stop them, American Jewish organizations continued

Failures to Rescue    69

to be sorely divided and to quarrel with one another. Joint Distribution Committee representatives Hyman and Leavitt were most unhappy with the World Jewish Congress' intervention in rescue work. They were most indignant that the Committee's name had been used in a commercial cable to Schwarzbart in London. (25) But when Kubowitzki suggested that a clearing house of representatives from the Committee, the World Jewish Congress, the Jewish Labor Committee and the Vaad Hahatzalah be created in order to unify the work of rescue, the Joint Distribution Committee representative said no. They would not collaborate with organizations that were involved with political activities, and they took occasion to "blast out against the Vaad Hahatzalah" (The Committee to Save the Jews) who they claimed were meddling in activities which were none of their concern. That fight took place on June 1, 1944. The next day, Rabbi Kotler of the Vaad had a few choice words for the Joint Distribution Committee. He reported that the Committee had "always followed a policy of strict legality" and that it resulted in great misfortune for many of Europe's Jews. He recalled that when some Polish Jews had fled to Wilno, the Joint Distribution Committee had refused to have anything to do with the people who had crossed the frontier illegally." And he reported that the Committee had refused to concern itself with people who had entered Portugal illegally.(26)

During these strife-torn discussions, the name of Lawrence Steinhardt was mentioned. A representative of the Vaad had information that Lawrence Steinhardt, as U.S. Ambassador to Moscow, had "behaved very badly" towards the Jewish people. He was "responsible for the misfortunes of hundreds of Jews," he had "inspired the ruthless policy of the State Department" and that perhaps his name would go down in infamy in the annals of Jewish history. Was the Vaad representative aware of the kind or reports Steinhardt, the American Jew, had sent to Assistant Secretary of State Breckinridge Long in 1941?(27) Did he know that Steinhardt had seemed thoroughly convinced that it was not in the interest of the United States to admit East European Jews? Did they know of the reports to Long?. Did they know that when American Jewish leaders had approached the President in 1941, and asked him to let more refugees into the United States, Roosevelt confronted them with Steinhardt's report?(28)

70   Failures to Rescue

The President of the United States said that he sympathized with the plight of the Jews, but he opposed the admission of Jews to America. Only extremely needy individuals would be admitted and then only if they passed rigorous admissions tests and if they would not in any way endanger United States security.(29) That was Franklin D. Roosevelt's policy and that was the essence of America's diplomacy of rescue. Because of such diplomacy, because of the Nazis and because of the division and sluggishness of Jewish leadership, some six million of our brothers and sisters were murdered in Europe.

Earlier proposals that the British parachute hundreds of Jewish volunteers into Hungary to help save the Jews had been approved by the British military as helpful to the Allied cause, but it was nevertheless, rejected by the Foreign and Colonial offices for political reasons.(30) What those technical difficulties and political reasons may have been is still not clear today. Perhaps the Allies did not want to see an end to extermination, because the more Jews who were exterminated, the less the Allies would have to concern themselves with the Jews after the war. Perhaps it all related to Anthony Eden's 1943 complaint that he would not know what to do with all the Jews if the Germans let them go.(31) Some officials like Adolph A. Berle rejected the suggestion that the U.N. threaten to select a German town and completely destroy it, for each Nazi atrocity. Berle ruled out such a procedure as being impracticable and claimed that all planes were needed for military objectives. Moreover, he maintained, that to impose such a threat would place the Allies "on a moral level with the Germans themselves." And Berle rejected any idea of urging the Germans to protest:

> ...on the one hand, the German people are not in any position to make any mass protest against the action of the Nazi rulers. On the other hand, we know that the Nazi leaders are continuously warning the German people, in order to stiffen their morale, that Germany's defeat will mean their massacre. For the U.N. to make any statement confirming that idea in the minds of the German people would seem to me most inadvisable as it would impel them to fight on with renewed desperation in support of their leaders....(32)

Secretary Edward R. Stettinius found it incredible that some military officials were opposed to helping the oppressed people.

If that was a true expression of military policy, said Stettinius to Hull, "we might as well shut up shop on trying to get additional refugees out of occupied Europe."(33)

He urged that the refugees be moved away from the theatres of combat and that facilities in North African camps be kept in liquid condition ready to receive more. If this were successfully accomplished, it would show the military that additional refugees would not strain their resources. In addition, he urged that the President should advise the military that rescue of refugees was an extremely important matter and "...in fact sufficiently important to require unusual effort on their part and to be set aside only for important military operational reasons."(34)

The rescue of Jews from Bulgaria and Romania in 1944-45 proved that if the Allies had wanted to, they could have saved many more. Moreover, during the **Gotterdammerung** of the Third Reich, German leaders like Heinrich Himmler were willing to exchange Jews for a mere promise of some special consideration at war's end. Goods, money and Swiss bank accounts no longer came into consideration. A few words could have saved hundreds of thousands, but they were not spoken. Did the Allies refuse to promise the Nazis anything because they did not wish to make false promises?

Special emissary Ira Hirschmann observed in March 1944, that a great deal more could have been accomplished had the War Refugee Board been created sooner.(35) But even the Balkan rescue of 1944 was of little consequence since the rescued had no place to go. The ships could be bought or rented, the Nazis could be bribed, but the free governments would not admit the refugees.

In December 1942, the Romanian government had approved a World Jewish Congress plan whereby the Bishop of Bucharest and the Papal Nuncio were to make shipping and other arrangements for the transport of 70,000 Jews to Tel Aviv under the Vatican flag. The Romanians had even offered to provide two ships. Later in March, 1943, the World Jewish Congress reported that Jews could be rescued from Romania and France if money for some Nazi leaders were placed in escrow in Swiss bank accounts. Rabbi Wise presented the plan to President Roosevelt saying that it would save thousands of lives and that the Allied armies could "see to it that these Nazi mercenaries shall not live to reap the benefit of their hostage and blackmailing plan." Roosevelt, Hull, and Morgenthau approved the negotiations and the granting of a license for the currency deal but many months of delay caused by the State Department and British officialdom prevented the completion of the transaction.(36)

Once the War Refugee Board was established, the Romanians were warned that a day of reckoning would come when those guilty of atrocities would be punished. Because they were afraid of the advancing Russian armies, they sought American friendship and they promised to cooperate. They agreed to release the 48,000 Jews in occupied Transnistria, end all forms of persecution, and permit 5,000 to leave for Palestine. One thing seemed to puzzle the Romanians: If the Jews meant so much to America, why had not America acted sooner?(37)

Again the answer was that the Allies did not want them. The British Government was against the ransom of Jews from the Balkans because it did not want them in Palestine and President Roosevelt insisted on a strict compliance with the immigration laws. When in March 1943, Foreign Minister Anthony Eden and Cordell Hull discussed the rescue of 60,000 Jews from the Balkans, Eden opposed:

> If we do that the Jews of the world will be wanting us to make a similar offer in Poland and Germany. Hitler might well take us up on such an offer and there simply are not enough ships...in the world to handle them. (38)

Eden claimed that the Jews were unacceptable since the Nazis would plant spies within their ranks.(39) The 1943 negotiations to save the Jews of the Balkans came to naught. Eden had his way.

On May 7, 1943, at the time of the Bermuda meeting, Secretary of State Hull wrote the President:

> I cannot recommend that we open the question of relaxing the provisions of our immigration laws and run the risk of a prolonged and bitter controversy in Congress on the immigration question - considering the generous quantity of refugees we have already received.
>
> I cannot recommend that we bring in refugees as temporary visitors....(40)

Roosevelt agreed with his Secretary of State as can be seen in the following memo dated May 14, 1943, which he sent to Hull:

> I do not think we can do other than comply strictly with the present immigration laws.
>
> I agree that North Africa may be used as a depot for those refugees but not a permanent resident without full approval of all authorities. I know, in fact, that there is plenty of room for them in North Africa....
>
> I agree with you that we cannot open the question of our immigration laws.
>
> I agree with you as to bringing in temporary visitors. We have already brought in a large number. (41)

In the summer of 1944, when the War Refugee Board intervened in Bulgaria, there were some forty-five thousand Jews to be saved in that country. Bulgarians responded to American pleas to save the Jews by asking that Allied bombings over Bulgaria be discontinued. Even though the Bulgarians received no assurances that the bombings would stop, they agreed to revoke their anti-Jewish laws and while German troops were still stationed in Bulgaria, they criticized the originators of discriminatory laws, declared themselves in favor of establishing a Jewish State in Palestine and promised to let Jews leave for Palestine. Like their Romanian neighbors, they feared the advancing Russian armies and they hoped that American forces would come to the Balkans to protect them.(42)

President Roosevelt had advised his people to keep on talking, for he claimed that the longer such talks would last, the more lives would be saved. The talks revealed that the Germans were ready to exchange Jews for trucks, food, cash or just a promise of leniency after the war. Allied talkers failed to give the Germans any positive response.

**A Jew Meets Himmler**

Some 80 kilometers outside Berlin, Norbert Mazur, a Jew representing the free world spoke with S.S. leader Heinrich Himmler in the manor library of Dr. Kersten, physician to Himmler, from 2:20 A.M. to 5 A.M. on Friday, April 20, 1945. Next to Hitler, Himmler was the most powerful man in Germany. He claimed that a month earlier he had issued a secret order which called for better treatment of Jews. He claimed that he had kept that order secret because of anti-Jewish feelings in Germany and because the Allies might have presumed Germany was ready to surrender. On that April morning, while Berlin lay in rubble, its roads filled with fleeing Germans and Allied planes flew over German skies unchallenged, Himmler sneaked out of Hitler's birthday party to negotiate with a Jew who represented the free world's last minute effort to save a few Jews. He sneaked out to inform a member of a people he had sought to destroy that in 1935 he had helped Jews leave Germany, and to complain that the Allies were spreading vicious atrocity stories. Himmler greeted Mazur a simple "good morning" and not with "Heil Hitler" and he said that he was glad Mazur had come. They then sat down at the table on which coffee was served.(43)

In a matter of fact way, the well dressed Himmler spoke of Germany's policies toward the Jews. He claimed that "...after the Nazis came to power, we wanted to solve this question once and for all, and I favored a humane solution through emigration. I negotiated with American organizations in order to effect a speedy immigration, but even those countries which professed to be friendly to the Jews did not want to let them in." He maintained that the Jews had been infested with typhus, that they helped the partisans and shot at German troops in the ghetto. He then claimed that the crematoriums had been built for reasons of health. "In order to check the epidemics, we were compelled to burn corpses of the innumerable persons carried off by these plagues. For this reason we had to build crematoriums, and of this circumstance they are now trying to fashion a noose for us." Himmler shrugged the concentration camps off by claiming that they got their bad reputation only because of their name. They should have been called "educational camps." But "it was not only Jews and political prisoners who were in these camps, but also common criminals who could not be released, even after the expiration of their sentences. As a result, Germany, even in a war year, had the lowest crime rate in decades." He promised better treatment for the Jews whom he constantly referred to as "Poles" because, according to the War Refugee Board papers, he had promised Hitler not to liberate any more "Jews."(44) There was no such differentiation to be found in Norbert Mazur's memorandum of conversation with Himmler.(45) Said Himmler:

> I keep Bergen-Belsen and Buchenwald in tact and what do I get as payment? Horrible untrue atrocity stories. (46)

After two and a half hours the interview came to an end. As Himmler left he said to Mazur: "The important part of the German people is going under with us; what happens to the rest does not matter."(47)

On May 8, 1945, Germany surrendered and the remnant of European Jewry was liberated. Some six million Jews were murdered by the German Nazis and their collaborators. There had been many possibilities of saving those six million from 1933 through 1945, but no free nation wanted them and so they were not saved. It appears that the so-called "free world" preferred to cover the facts and permit the exterminations to continue. Even the last minute efforts of the War Refugee Board were without real meaning for there was no place for the rescued to go. President Roosevelt had asked neutrals, Latin Americans, the Pope, Mussolini, and many others to give Jews some kind of asylum, but he would not ask his State Department or the Congress to ease up on the immigration restrictions, nor did he wish to disturb the British position in the Middle East. The British kept Erez Israel, or Palestine as they called it, closed to the Jews and thereby sealed their doom in Europe. There was lots of diplomacy, but little rescue. The Jewish people were divided and they were dependent upon the good graces of others. Perhaps they learned as did the world that they could not depend upon others for help, but that they could only depend on themselves and God. No one else would help. They might have learned that without a united determination to help themselves, they would be lost. That was an expensive lession. It cost the lives of six million Jewish people.

As Dr. Gerhard Riegner put it to me in an interview: "Hitler's greatest triumph was the fact that no one wanted the Jews. That was the worst of all," and "if Jewry had been united and accepted the Peel Plan of 1936 (for Partition of Palestine) we could have had something...."(48) If.

## 76  Failures to Rescue

1  A. Weissberg, *Desperate Mission: Joel Brand Story* (New York, 1958), 53-61. Hereafter cited as *Desperate Mission*.

2  Nora Levin, *The Holocaust, The Destruction of European Jewry 1933-1945* (New York, 1973) 538-539. Hereafter cited as Levin, *Holocaust*

3  Eichmann Trial District Court Jerusalem Criminal Case No. 40/61 May 29, 30, 1961. File No. 56 and No. 57. Hereafter cited as *Eichmann Trial*.

4  *Eichmann Trial*

5  *Ibid.*

6  *Ibid.*

7  W.R.B., May 25, 1944, 865; *Desperate Mission*, 105, 152. Steinhardt's letter found in the World Jewish Congress Archives:"Two days ago an individual by name Joel Brand documented as the representative of the Jewish Community of Budapest, arrived in Istanbul and submitted to Barlas of the Jewish Agency a proposal which it is said originated with...Eichmann to the effect that in exchange for 2 million cakes of soap ...Eichmann would agree to stop the deportation and extermination."

8  *Desperate Mission*, 157-158, 163-165.

9  *Ibid.*, 152-153.

10  Ira A. Hirschman, *Lifeline to a Promised Land* (New York, 1946) 115. His books must be read carefully and with caution. During one of several interviews I had with him in New York, he claimed that he had advised the U.S. against trading trucks for Jews.

11  Burton Y. Berry to Secretary of State, Letter Report, June 13, 1944, State Department File No. 862.20200/ 6-1344, National Archives, Washington, D.C.

12  Moshe Sharett wrote to Nahum Goldmann on July 8, 1944:"... Brandt should be enabled to return immediately...in order not to give unnecessary excuse to the enemy." This letter found in World Jewish Congress Archives, New York.

13  W.R.B., June 9, 19; July 7, 28, 1944, 866-876.

14  *Ibid.*, August 22; October 6, 1944, 799-814.

15  I. Schwartzbart to Stanislaw Mikolajzyk, June 27, 1944, World Jewish Congress, New York.

16  A. Leon Kubowitzki to John Pehle, July 1, 1944, World Jewish Congress, New York.

17  *Ibid*.

18  W.R.B., June 24; July 4, 1944, 750, 767; *Unity in Dispersion, A History of the World Jewish Congress* (New York, 1948), 167.

19  *Eichmann Trial*.

20  *Ibid*.

21  John J. McCloy to A.L. Kubowitzki, September 3, 1944, World Jewish Congress, New York.

22  A.L. Kubowitzki to Kaperstein, October 1, 1944, World Jewish Congress, New York.
23  *Ibid.*
24  A.L. Kubowitzki to John J. McCloy, October 4, 1944, World Jewish Congress, New York.
25  Note dated June 9, 1944, on the June 2, 1944 conference of the World Jewish Congress and J.D.C. reps., World Jewish Congress, New York.
26  *Ibid.*
27  Steinhardt to Breckinridge Long, May 8, 1941, B. Long Papers, The Library of Congress. See B. Long's Memo of September 5, 1940, and B. Long's Diary of November 27, 1941.
28  B. Long Diary, October 10, 1940; Minutes of the President's Advisory Committee on Political Refugees, October 30, 1940, Stephen S. Wise Papers, Brandeis University.
29  *Ibid.*
30  *Eichmann Trial*
31  *Foreign Relations of the United States,* March 27, 1943, III, 38-39.
32  A.A. Berle to B. Long, April 23, 1943, B. Long Papers, Library of Congress. In 1941, Mrs. Roosevelt met with Jacob Rosenheim, M.G. Tress and M. Schenkowlewski who proposed that the White House recognize the Jews of Europe as prisoners of war. But Mrs. Roosevelt rejected the idea because it might force the U.S. to retaliate on German prisoners of war. The Germans would then retaliate against American prisoners and it would all lead to more murder. Conversation between Mrs. Roosevelt, J. Rosenheim, M.G. Tress and M. Schenkowlewski, Eleanor Roosevelt File, October 14, 1941, James MacDonald Papers, Columbia University.
33  Edward R. Stettinius, Jr. to Secretary of State, January 8, 1944, Breckinridge Long Papers, The Library of Congress.
34  *Ibid.*
35  Memo dated March 6, 1944, in Lawrence Steinhardt Papers, The Library of Congress. Interview with Ira Hirschmann.
36  Blum, *Years of War,* 207-223.
37  Ira Hirschmann, *Caution to the Winds* (New York, 1962), 156-160.
38  *Foreign Relations of the United States,* March 27, 1943, III 38-9.
39  *Ibid.*
40  *Ibid.,* May 7, 1943, I 176-178.
41  *Ibid.,* May 14, 1943, I, 179.
42  W.R.B. August 7; September 26, 1944, 834-837.
43  W.R.B., March 28; April 25, 1945, 921-927. Norbert Mazur Memorandum of conversation with Himmler undated. World Jewish Congress Archives, New York.
44  *Ibid.*

78  Failures to Rescue

45  *Ibid.*
46  *Ibid.*
47  *Ibid.*
48  Interview with Dr. Gerhard Riegner, April 20, 1973.

# CHAPTER V

## The 982

Throughout his Presidency, Franklin D. Roosevelt was unwilling to fight the Congress and public opinion to end the restrictive immigration laws and regulations. Involved in much talk, the President made many promises and sent his representatives to many conferences that examined the immigration question. From Evian 1938 to Bermuda 1943, while Jews were exterminated, the Allies conferred, talked and continued to exclude Palestine as a place of refuge. Many words were spoken but little action was taken.

When individuals like Bernard M. Baruch urged President Roosevelt to get the U.N. to care for one million refugees (1) the President responded by asking all nations to open their borders, if only temporarily, to the victims of Nazi oppression. He warned that "all those who share the guilt shall share the punishment," and he appealed to all freedom loving nations to "rally to this righteous undertaking." The appeal of March 24, 1944, was very moving. But while the President appealed to the free world to open its gates, some Americans asked Roosevelt to do the same thing. The Emergency Committee to Save the Jews, which included among its membership Dean Alfange, Will Rogers, Jr., Louis Bromfield and Ben Hecht, asked the President to create "free ports" in America, Palestine and Africa. Many members of Congress, including Vito Marcantonio, of the Italo-American community in East Harlem, New York, likewise asked Roosevelt to establish "free ports" as sanctuaries for Jews.

It was hard to understand how the U.S. could transport thousands of German prisoners of war across the Atlantic, but could not try to save some of the persecuted. But while in November, 1943, Secretary of the Treasury Henry J. Morgenthau, Jr. urged the President to accept the "Refugee-P.O.W." concept which had the support of Congress(2), others like Secretary of War Henry L. Stimson opposed the idea, claiming that the President had no right to subvert the immigration laws and quotas and to act unilaterally on a matter which "concerns a very deeply held feeling of our people."(3)

Roosevelt decided in favor of the "free port" idea. He asked that a group be selected representing the various persecuted peoples that had fled to southern Italy. On June 12, 1944, D-Day plus six, the White House announced its decision to create a "free port" in the U.S. for some 1,000 people and it asked that other nations help in the rescue of Hitler's victims. The Nazis said Roosevelt, were persevering in their extermination policies to "salvage from military defeat, victory for nazi principles - the very principles which this war must destroy unless we shall have fought in vain." He recalled that in January 1944, the War Refugee Board was created to save those in danger of extermination and protect those who could not escape. Few were saved. Many still faced death at the hands of a "fiendish extermination campaign" in German occupied territories. In keeping with the American tradition of "liberty and justice," Roosevelt declared, the U.S. would admit one thousand refugees on a temporary basis. At the same time he reassured all concerned that the group would not present a security risk for they would be placed in a vacated army camp on the Atlantic coast "under appropriate security restrictions."

> Accordingly, arrangements have been made to bring immediately to this country approximately 1,000 refugees who have fled from their homelands to southern Italy. Upon the termination of the war they will be sent back to their homeland. These refugees are predominantly women and children. They will be placed on their arrival in a vacated army camp on the Atlantic coast where they will remain under appropriate security restrictions.(4)

On August 3, 1944, 982 displaced persons representing seventeen nationalities, arrived in New York City after a difficult journey on board a U.S. Navy ship that was part of a large convoy. Once they arrived in Fort Ontario, Oswego, New York, they were kept under strict military surveillance. They were almost as closely guarded as the German prisoners of war. They had traveled across the Atlantic to find liberty, but all they found was eighteen months of confinement.

When a group of the refugees asked Rabbi Stephen S. Wise to convince Roosevelt to release them from the camp, the Rabbi replied that he had little influence with the President, and that F.D.R. did not listen to his advice. Rabbi Wise believed that a time would come when F.D.R. would ask for his advice, but then it would be too late.(5)

William O'Dwyer - War Refugee Board chief - suggested that the refugees be permitted "to reside in normal communities throughout the United States" but Attorney General Francis Biddle insisted that they remain in Fort Ontario because he felt that if they were released there would be widespread opposition in Congress and further rescue operations would be seriously hampered.(6) Biddle was "opposed to any arrangement being made whereby they could obtain status under the immigration laws. Such an arrangement would in my opinion, be a breach of faith to the Congress."(7)

Strongly opposed to the whole project, some individuals like Senator Robert R. Reynolds wanted to know on what grounds F.D.R. chose to disregard the law and immigration quotas. Frances Biddle explained that the project was outside the purview of the immigration laws and the refugees were not immigrants, but only temporary visitors. Moreover, prisoners of war were being detained in America on the same basis, and military necessity in Italy required the "temporary disposition" of the 982.(8)

Some were afraid that the country would be flooded with starving Jews and that subsequently America would be ruined. President Roosevelt reassured those concerned that America had taken in the refugees and "parked them at Fort Ontario" only temporarily, and that they would "have to go back after the war."

One still wonders what motivated President Roosevelt to invite the 982. Was it to inspire others to follow the American example or was it only to silence those who claimed that the Allies would rather have seen Jews murdered than admit them to their shores? The sad experience of World War II taught many that they could not rely upon the so-called "civilized" impulses of the world.(9)

The Jews learned that their best chance was self-reliance, and so they continued to fight for the rebirth of Israel.

1   Bernard M. Baruch to F.D.R., January 8, 1944, President's Official File 3186, F.D.R. Library, Hyde Park, N.Y.
2   Memo dated November 4, 1943, President's Official File, 5450, F.D.R. Library, Hyde Park, N.Y.
3   Henry L. Stimson to F.D.R., Letter May 8, 1944, President's Official File, 3186, Hyde Park, N.Y.
4   *Congressional Record,* June 12, 1944, page 5079.
5   Interview with one of the 982. The individual preferred to remain anonymous.
6   *History of the War Refugee Board with Selected Documents,* January 22, 1944 - September 15, 1945, March 1, 1945, 950. Hereafter cited as *W.R.B.*
7   Biddle to J.P. Chamberlain, J.P. Chamberlain Papers, Yivo Institute, New York.
8   *W.R.B.,* June 14, 1944, 948-950.
9   In an interview with H. Katzki, a J.D.C. executive, I asked why there were not any other Oswegos. His answer on June 16, 1971, was that the war was soon over and that there was "no need for them." A very strange answer in view of the condition of the camps in which the refugees found themselves after the war until 1948. See Y. Bauer, *Flight and Rescue: Brichah* (New York, 1970).

# CHAPTER VI

# To The Promised Land

There was one place that could have received the Jews. That place was Erez Israel or Palestine, as the British and Romans liked to call it. By May 1939, the British closed it to Jews. Only 75,000 could enter between 1939 and 1945. The British closed Erez Israel and the Roosevelt Administration went along with that policy. The British violated their pledges, made to the Jewish people since the time of Lord Arthur Balfour, and President Roosevelt collaborated in that violation.

**Background to the White Paper Policy**

Americans and their governments had displayed a traditional interest in the establishment of a Jewish Homeland in Erez Israel since the days of President James Monroe. Every President from Woodrow Wilson's time declared his support for the establishment of such a state.

In November 1917, many had hoped that the Balfour Declaration issued by the British Government in support of the establisment of a Jewish Homeland in Erez Israel (both sides of the Jordan) might signal the end of the diaspora because it was soon confirmed by the Allied governments, and it formed the basis for the League of Nations Mandate over the Palestine area. In his letter to Lord Rothschild, the British Foreign Secretary declared:

> His Majesty's Government view with favour the establishment in Palestine of a national home for the Jewish people and will use their best endeavors to facilitate the achievement of this object, it being clearly understood that nothing shall be done which may prejudice the civil and religious rights of existing non-Jewish communities in Palestine, or the rights and political status enjoyed by Jews in any other country.

That declaration may never have been issued had President Wilson not urged the British Government to issue it.

Presidential support for a Jewish Homeland continued even during the isolationist period of the 1920s and 1930s. In 1922, Henry Cabot Lodge, a leading isolationist Senator, led the Senate in support of a Joint Congressional resolution favoring the establishment of a Jewish Homeland, and President Warren G. Harding signed that resolution. On October 29, 1932, President Herbert Hoover praised the work of the Zionists in Palestine: "I have watched with genuine admiration the steady and unmistakable progress made in the rehabilitation of Palestine which...is renewing its youth and vitality through the enthusiasm, hard work and self-sacrifice of the Jewish pioneers ..." But while Presidents and Congress maintained a traditional sympathy for Zionism, the State Department consistently opposed even expressions of sympathy in favor of Zionism, presumably because it feared possible Arab disapproval.

President Roosevelt's policy towards the question of a Jewish Homeland or State in Erez Israel was two-faced. To the Jews, he would say that he supported the idea and to the Arabs he would say that nothing would be done without their consultation, and he thereby gave the Arab sheiks a veto over the whole matter. This was similar to his policy towards the rescue of European Jewry. F.D.R. would declare his sympathy for the plight of the Jews, but would not make a move to open up America to those Jews who might escape the Nazi murderers.

In the early 1930s, President Roosevelt issued many statements and proclamations in support of Zionism. By promising to "watch with deep sympathy the progress of Palestine," he recalled how American Presidents and the Congress had supported the idea of making Palestine into a Jewish land. He maintained that the Jews had the right to rebuild their land based on the principle that all people had the inalienable right to life, liberty and the pursuit of happiness. He found it "a source of renewed hope and courage," that through international understanding, Jews could return to their promised land, "to resettle the land where their faith was born and from which much of our modern civilization has emanated."(1)

His words were many and beautiful, but his deeds were few and empty.

President Roosevelt was unwilling to inhibit British imperialist ambitions in the Middle East, and he refused to upset the Arab sheiks for fear of undermining Allied military efforts during World War II. He had a Balfour Declaration to uphold. A Balfour Declaration issued by Britain thanks to the support of President Woodrow Wilson, and which was upheld by American Presidents since 1917.(2) He had to uphold the promise that Palestine would be made into a Jewish Homeland, but he did not uphold it. While he issued proclamations in support of a Jewish Homeland and expressed the hope that the Jews could return to Erez Israel, he, at the same time, reassured the Arabs that nothing would transpire without their consent and he suggested to Zionist leaders that the Jews look elsewhere for a homeland.

When the Peel Report of 1936, calling for the Partition of West Palestine, proved unacceptable to both Jews and Arabs and there were very definite indications that the British planned to impose severe restrictions on Jewish immigration to Erez Israel, President Roosevelt revealed his usual favorable attitude towards the Jewish Homeland idea by declaring that Jews could make Erez Israel into the "eastern Mediterranean." But in terms of specific steps, all F.D.R. did was to tell the British that America wished to be informed of any changes in policy involving Palestine.(3)

It was no secret by the Fall, 1937, that the British planned to limit Jewish immigration to Palestine to less than 12,000 per year. When the British asked the State Department for information regarding Jewish attitudes towards Palestine, Wallace Murray, Chief of the State Department's Near East Division, told them that the Jews were badly split. Rabbi Wise and his supporters wanted complete freedom of Jewish immigration to Palestine while non-Zionist Jews, such as Felix Warburg, were opposed to the establishment of a Jewish Homeland in Palestine for fear that such immigration might damage their position and standing throughout the rest of the world and lead to widespread anti-Semitism. Still another faction accepted partition in the hope that more favorable terms might be achieved through future negotiations with the British.(4) Wallace Murray observed on September 17, 1937, that in "view of this clear division of opinion among the representatives of American Jewry it seems to me that we are in a strong position to request that they come to some agreement among themselves before they approach us with a view to our taking any particular line of action. In other words we seem to be in good position to ask Rabbi Wise to produce some proof that he speaks on behalf of all of American Jewry before we comply with any specific requests that he may make."(5) This was an impossible request.

American Jewry, and for that matter Jewry throughout the world, was divided on the future goals for Palestine. Some favored partition and the creation of an independent Jewish state. Others opposed partition because they wanted all of Palestine, and still others were totally opposed to a Jewish state. The Jews were as divided on the question of the future state as they were on the rescue of European Jewry, as they had been divided throughout history. This division enabled F.D.R. and certain State Department officials like Wallace Murray to find further excuses for not taking effective steps to fulfill previous U.S. commitments. It was easy for Murray to say "first come to some agreement amongst yourselves and then come to us."

Throughout the war years, the anti-Zionist Jews continued to present their view to the Roosevelt people. On September 25, 1943, Morris D. Waldman, Executive Vice President of the American Jewish Committee, wrote to Wallace Murray that "...the promise of a Jewish political nationhood flies in the face of 2,000 years of Jewish history; that it is a denial of the rights won by Jews since their emancipation; that the theory and existence of a World Jewish Congress is a singular innovation in international affairs and that threatens to work damaging effect upon the status of Jews in all countries; that it is especially obnoxious to American Jews because it is repugnant to the spirit of American democracy which tolerates variety only in religious and cultural institutions but does not tolerate racial and religious political minorities; a democracy that encourages religious, racial and cultural loyalties but does not suffer hyphenated or divided political allegiance."(6)

Four days later Waldman pleaded his case personally to Murray. He was convinced that it was time to organize and to express the viewpoint of the great majority of American Jews who, he felt, "opposed and feared Jewish nationalism in any form because of the danger that the position of Jews in the United States was becoming seriously undermined."(7)

...the American Jewish Committee would take a highly important decision to organize American Jews for the purpose of actively opposing all manifestations, whether on the part of Zionists, the American Committee for a Jewish Army, or others, which would tend to set off American Jews from other American citizens.(8)

Waldman, in conversations with Murray and other State Department officials in January 1944, maintained that within a year or two, the majority of Jewish opinion in America would be anti-Zionist. According to a Near East Division memo found in the Long Papers, he planned to bring about this conversion through publicity in Jewish papers, and local representatives in Jewish communities. Waldman claimed that "the first generation eastern European Jews in the U.S. were now a dwindling minority and that their children were in his opinion good Americans who were not likely to be carried away by notions of extreme Jewish nationalism."(9) Moreover, he maintained, that if the Zionist activities were permitted to continue "a greatly increased anti-Semitic movement in the country (would) arise after the war, with far-reaching and disasterous consequences."(10)

Waldman's views reflected the position taken by the American Jewish Committee at this time towards Palestine. While it favored an end to the restrictions imposed by the White Paper policy of 1939, it was opposed to a Jewish State idea. Its leadership was afraid that a Jewish State might cause American Jews embarassment. They were afraid that the anti-Semites might have more fuel for their furnaces of hate. They were afraid of being asked: Are you Americans or are you members of the Jewish State? As the American Jewish Committee stipulated in its summary position on November 8, 1943: "...there can be no political identification of Jews outside of Palestine with whatever government may be there established."(11) That position would change once Israel became a reality. To date, the American Jewish Committee supports the State of Israel.

Richard E. Gutstadt, Director of the Anti-Defamation League, wrote to Justice Louis Brandeis on August 16, 1940, of his fears concerning charges of divided loyalties as a result of Zionism.(12) Justice Brandeis had an answer for such unwarranted fears:

> Let no American imagine that Zionism is inconsistent with Patriotism. Multiple loyalties are objectionable only if they are inconsistent. A man is a better citizen of the U.S. for being also a loyal citizen of his state, and of his city....Every American Jew who aids in advancing the Jewish settlement in Palestine though he feels that neither he nor his descendants will ever live there, will likewise be a better man and a better American for doing so.

The American Jewish community was badly divided on the question of Palestine and rescue, and American Jews were afraid to speak up lest they be accused of warmongering and disloyalty. This made it much easier for U.S. officials to disregard the plight of European Jewry and to go along with British colonial ambitions in the Middle East.

One of the most tragic aspects of this history was that American Jews like Rosenberg, Steinhardt and Waldman were leaders in the American Jewish community, and some revealed the same kind of bias towards the persecuted Jews of Europe as did some Jews in Austria and Germany when Jews from Poland entered their countries after World War I. Those Austrian and German Jews of the 1920s exhibited nothing less than Jewish anti-Semitism, and their anti-Semitism added to the virulent anti-Semitism of such misfits as Eugen Duhring, Joseph P. Chamberlain, Julius Streicher, Karl Lueger and Adolf Hitler. Individuals like Steinhardt and Waldman seemed to have conveniently forgotten that they had been immigrants, the sons of immigrants, or at the very most the grandsons of immigrants. And their biased attitudes contributed to the abysmal failure that was the diplomacy of rescue.

Perhaps Roosevelt did not want to upset the shakey British Empire and then be required to bail it out, or perhaps it was because he did not think Palestine was suitable for mass Jewish immigration - whatever his reasons - he suggested to Rabbi Wise that Jews look elsewhere. Roosevelt felt that if war could be postponed "for another two or three years at most, we will have a world conference on re-allocation of territories....and then we might find some large areas as a second choice for the Jews." Roosevelt did not seem to understand or did not want to understand the importance of Erez Israel to the Jewish people. The President saw that it was so small an area, a country so tough and difficult to cultivate and an area so touchy politically. It would be much more sensible to locate a land with fewer difficulties. Rabbi Wise asked the President if he would care to swap the few hundred acres of Hyde Park for the one and a half million acres of the King Ranch of Texas. "No, I would not," answered the President, "but I might be glad to have both." The President denied intimating that the Jews give up Palestine, but being a practical man he realized the necessity of having alternative plans. He was not suggesting that the Jews give up Palestine "but Palestine possibilities are going to be exhausted so you ought to have another card up your sleeve."(13)

According to a letter dated November 16, 1938, written by Justice Brandeis to Robert Szold, the President posed a similar question to him, "You don't object to satellites?" "No," replied the Justice, "but Palestine alone can provide the remedy." Brandeis advised Roosevelt that at one time he believed the world's indignation at Hitler's atrocities would eventually compel Britain to permit Jews to enter Palestine, but he gave up that idea and became convinced that only strength and numbers in Palestine could make the British keep the promises with respect to Palestine. The world had to realize that Erez Israel could absorb the Jewish refugees. If there were other countries which offered refuge, very well and good; but Erez Israel was the foremost goal.(14)

In October 1938, Chaim Weizmann advised leading Americans to persuade the President to prevent the British from blocking Jewish immigration and establishing an Arab state in Palestine. Do not "submit to the fate of the Assyrians and give up Jewish Palestine," pleaded Weizmann.(15) And in early March 1939, he approached F.D.R. directly and asked him to stop the British from breaking their solemn trust. Such a breach, warned Weizmann, was bound to produce catastrophe in Palestine and would "completely undermine all confidence in international pledges given small nations." He believed that at this "zero hour" for the Jews, only the President's influence could stop British plans to establish a new state where Jews would remain a permanent minority and only the President of the United States could keep the doors of Erez Israel open.(16) A month later, Weizmann asked Brandeis to intervene with the President:

> ...induce President urge British Government delay publication their proposals....If new policy imposed Jews will conduct immigration disregard legal restrictions. Will settle land without permission even if exposed British bayonets.
>
> Please impress President...only extraordinary emphatic step can possibly produce effect.(17)

Brandeis, Wise and others went to see the President in 1938, and in 1939, but they were unable to change the Administration's thinking, and on May 15, 1939, the British issued their White Paper which provided that after a five year period when 75,000 Jews were to enter Palestine, the Arabs would be consulted about future Jewish immigration. Acquisition of lands by Jews was to be severely restricted. The British officially declared their opposition to the creation of a "Jewish state against the will of the Arab population of the country." No restrictions were imposed on the number of Arabs that could enter Erez Israel. And many thousands did immigrate to Erez Israel at this time. The British went along with the Arab terrorist leaders of the area like Haj Amin el Husseini, whom they had made the Mufti of Jerusalem with a salary of $500,000 per year. British officials had used their diplomatic umbrella once again - this time over Erez Israel. By making a scrap of paper out of Lord Balfour's promise to the Jews, they closed the only place of refuge for millions of European Jews.(18) International politicians and their diplomacy had condemned the Jews of Europe to the gas chambers of Nazi Germany.

After the British came out with their infamous White Paper of 1939, Roosevelt seemed unwilling to accept Britain's interpretation that the Palestine Mandate framers had not intended to make Palestine into a Jewish state, but he did not fight it. Said F.D.R.:

> Frankly, I do not believe that the British are wholly correct in saying that the framers of the Palestine Mandate "could not have intended that Palestine should be converted into a Jewish state against the will of the Arab population of the country.
>
> Frankly, I do not see how the British Govt. reads into the original Mandate or into the White Paper of 1922 any policy that would limit Jewish immigration.(19)

Roosevelt promised Wise that he would do all he could,(20) but when the rabbi asked Secretary of State Cordell Hull to convince the British to postpone implementation of the White Paper, Hull insisted that he had already done all he could. Hull even refused to issue a public statement of concern with British policy maintaining that such a declaration could be made only if America were willing to participate in a mandate over Palestine. Claiming that Congress would throw him out of a window if he ever made such a proposal, Hull informed Wise that it had been one of his "deepest disappointments that after marshalling every influence we possessed the British Government should have issued the White Paper."(21)

As Wise put it to Hull, "moral right" had "given way to political expediency."(22) The international politicians or diplomats had condemned the Jews to permanent exile, and the gas chambers. The German Nazis operated the murder camps, but it was Britain and her friends that furnished the inmates by preventing them to escape to such places of refuge as Erez Israel.

**The Jewish Army**
The Zionist answer to the British White Paper was illegal immigration - **Aliyah Bet** - and the formation of a Jewish Army. Zionists like David Ben Gurion proposed that at least a million Jewish immigrants come to Israel and present the British with a *fait accompli* - a strong and powerful Jewish Army. Writing to Brandeis he said that we can "depend...only on ourselves."(23) When the war erupted in Europe, Ben Gurion advised his fellow Zionists not to expect a reversal in British foreign policy, but to concentrate on bringing young Jews to Erez Israel, acquire more land and build a great united Jewish army as a new and major factor in the Middle East. By helping the British fight the Nazis, he believed, the Jews could gain self-respect and eventually establish their own independent state. Unless the help was given, he felt, it would not be possible to "absolve the Jewish people in the judgement of history from their failure to contribute to the destruction of the greatest enemy that ever arose against the very existence of the Jewish people."(24)

But again, American Jews were timorous. They could not muster enough gumption to help the Jews of Israel form a strong Jewish Army. When Zionist Revisionist leader Vladimir Jabotinsky came to New York in March 1940, to help promote the Jewish Army, he found a timid and fearful group of Jewish leaders. He had "never seen American Jewry so scared of local anti-Semitism as they are now that the danger seems really tangible and widespread."(25)

The Yishuv wanted to arm itself and to fight for survival. Rabbi Wise urged President Roosevelt to help. But Roosevelt said it was the business of the British. He advised Wise on June 9, 1941, that the "first lines of defense for Palestine are in outlying areas, and it is my distinct impression that the British are using all their available arms and other equipment in the various active zones."(26) The President insisted that the British had to have the support of both the Arabs and the Jews.(27)

Some 125,000 Yishuv Jews volunteered to join the British Army. There was no such volunteering from the Arabs. Haj Amin el Husseini collaborated with the Germans. The Iraqis collaborated with the Germans. The Syrians collaborated with the Germans, as did many Egyptians. Only after four years of pleading and insisting were the Jews of Erez Israel able to achieve at least part of their goal - Jewish units with Hebrew as the official language. This deserves a separate and complete chapter, but in brief, by September 1944, the British finally announced the creation of a Jewish Brigade. Within one month, the Brigade was fighting in Italy against the Nazis. After the fighting stopped in Europe, Jews of Erez Israel worked to liberate their fellow Jews from Europe, and they helped bring them to Erez.

### The Illegals

The British stopped at nothing to prevent Jewish immigration into Palestine. They used every conceivable device to end Jewish immigration. They even went so far as to claim that the immigrants were Nazi agents. The British and the Roosevelt Administration both opposed Jewish immigration to Palestine. Both catered to the Arabs.

In June of 1943, Chaim Weizmann spoke to Roosevelt, and as in February 1940, he presented a plan of settlement suggested by H. St. John Philby,(28) whereby Jews and Arabs would settle their differences peacefully. Accordingly, a joint Anglo-American guarantee would insure Jewish settlement in Palestine and a resettlement of Arab displaced persons would take place for which the Jews would pay the Arabs some twenty million Pounds Sterling, and all the Arab states would achieve independence.(29)

President Roosevelt seemed agreeable. He felt that perhaps a little "bakshish" might encourage a settlement with the Arabs, but before approaching King Ibn Saud of Saudi Arabia, he consulted with the British. The British approved, providing no suggestions were made prejudicing the interests of the Arab states and provided the conversations were purely exploratory. (30) Roosevelt sent the pro-Arab and pro-British Colonel Halford L. Hoskins on this mission.

Hoskins came back with a very negative account. He reported King Saud as saying that unless a Federation were created which would include Lebanon, Syria, Trans-Jordan and a bi-national Palestinian state, there would be war between Arabs and Jews. Moreover, Hoskins claimed that Saud would not talk with Weizmann because he was insulted by the idea of a bribe. Saud felt "impugned" by the attempt to bribe him with twenty million Pounds Sterling, guaranteed by President Roosevelt.(31)

Roosevelt disclaimed any knowledge of such a suggestion.(32) But in a memorandum written by David K. Niles to President Truman, a number of years later, Niles recalled that Roosevelt had told him privately "he could do anything that was needed to be done with Ibn Saud with a few million dollars."(33) According to Weizmann, Philby had maintained that Saud would have accepted the proposals if Hoskins had not bungled it. Saud's angry outbursts against Weizmann were really directed against Hoskins' bungling.(34) The attitude of the Roosevelt people and the British was entirely too gloomy and pessimistic to reconcile differences between Arabs and Jews. Their personal predilictions and bungling interventions prevented peace between Jews and Arabs.

The approach to Saud failed, but according to Nahum Goldmann, Winston Churchill promised Weizmann that he would soon abandon the White Paper policy in favor of fulfilling the Balfour Declaration. After crushing Hitler "the Allies will have to establish the Jews in the position where they belong." Recalling how much trouble the Arabs had caused the Allies during the war, Churchill reassured Weizmann that the Jews would get his support, and that he "would bite deep into the problem and it is going to be the biggest plum of the war."(35)  Thus in January 1944, Zionists had British reassurances of support(36) and in February the same British Government helped persuade Roosevelt to kill a Congressional resolution which called for the establishment of a Jewish Commonwealth in Palestine.(37)

At least three years before Zionist leaders like Ben Gurion and Weizmann called for an end to using the delicate touch with British and American officials.  Meeting with Zionist leaders of America in December 1940, Ben Gurion called for the creation of a unified Zionist policy.  "We cannot live from hand to mouth and by a policy I mean...a clear objective or objectives in the immediate future, during the war and at the end of the war...."(38)  On July 17, 1944, Chaim Weizmann insisted that the Zionist movement openly declare its goals.  As he spoke to a meeting of fellow Zionists in America, he stated that "whatever the Arabs will have will be due to the efforts of England and America, so that if England and America really both had political acumen, courage and desire to settle the Jewish problem decently, they can do it now."  The Zionists must make it "clear to England and America what they have to do in order to bring about what I call a decent solution to the Jewish problem."  Erez should absorb "within...20 years...about three million Jews, particularly the younger generation."(39) He proposed a confederation with the Arabs, and he called for an open declaration of Zionist demands. Nahum Goldmann, among others, was opposed.  This, argued Goldmann, would give the Arabs much more of "a nuisance value than they have had...."(40)  Goldmann wanted to wait until the Allied victory would be at hand.  Weizmann told Goldmann that he was merely echoing the British line and thanks to people like him "...the British...have got us where they want us."  The British had created a climate of opinion that nothing could be done to embarass them since they were at war: "You Jews are interested that we should win the war and therefore sit tight." by July 1941, Weizmann was no longer willing to sit tight.  Nor was he willing to accept the argument that only the Arabs had a nuisance value. Weizmann wanted to create a "Jewish nuisance value."  It was about time that the British stopped playing with the White Paper and the Arab question.  "For two years we sat tight and swallowed every possible ignominy.  We did not want to embarass them. But we believe we have a contribution to make to victory and this contribution is that they should know the truth and that they should know what we want to do for the Jews in Palestine."(41)

By 1942, a conference was held. It was called the Biltmore Conference because it was held at the Hotel Biltmore in New York. There the Zionist dream of reestablishing the Jewish Homeland was openly declared for all to know. But the Roosevelt Administration - supporting the British position in the Middle East - fought tooth and nail against having even a Congressional resolution in support of a Jewish Homeland in Erez Israel.

Secretary of War Henry L. Stimson advised Congress that a Congressional resolution might prejudice the American war effort. Army Chief of Staff George C. Marshall refused to be responsible for the military complications in the Moslem world if the pro-Zionist resolutions were passed by Congress. Secretary of State Hull warned that the resolutions would inhibit negotiations with King Saud.(42) The Congress yielded.

Members of Congress accepted the line that Congressional resolutions in favor of a Jewish State might be used as propaganda by the Nazis to injure the Allied military position, and that the U.N. would have to devote its energies to keeping Arabs and Jews from killing one another. Breckinridge Long had persuaded the Members of Congress that while Roosevelt was trying to convince the British to change their White Paper policy, the President hoped that discussion could be postponed until after the war so that the United Nations could deal with the problem, and the U.S. would not need to shoulder the responsibility alone. Or as John J. McCloy, Assistant Secretary of Defense, the same individual who opposed the bombing of death camps, would say, "from a military point of view, we would much prefer to let such sleeping dogs lie."(43)

The official policy of F.D.R. was not at all satisfactory to the Jewish community, a community that was now bordering on hysteria because of the murder of millions of their brethren in Europe. Roosevelt's expressions of good will would no longer suffice. The leadership provided by such individuals as Rabbi Abba Hillel Silver challenged Rabbi Wise and his group. In conversations with State Department officials, Rabbi Silver demanded to know what he should tell his people. How much longer must the Jews defer? Silver proposed that Roosevelt, at least, issue a statement saying that the cause was just. (44) State Department officials rejected Silver's suggestion. But on March 2, 1944, Roosevelt congratulated Henrietta Szold for her work with Youth Aliyah.(45) And despite strong State Department objections, the President complied with Rabbi Silver's request for a statement of support. Roosevelt authorized Wise and Silver, on March 16, 1944, to issue the following declaration on his behalf:

> The President has authorized us to say that the American Government has never given its approval to the White Paper of 1939. The President expressed his conviction that when future decisions are reached, full justice will be done to those who seek a Jewish National Home, for which our Government and the American people have always had the deepest sympathy, today more than ever in view of the tragic plight of hundreds of thousands of homeless Jewish refugees.(46)

Shortly thereafter, the Roosevelt people would reassure the Arabs that no decision would be made without full consultation with both Arabs and Jews.

**The Last Days of F.D.R.**

Roosevelt privately confided to Wise in January - March 1945, that he had given too much consideration to King Ibn Saud's power and to poor advice from the State Department and British Colonial Office. He said he wanted to see a Jewish State created in Palestine. If necessary "we will build a fence around Palestine to keep the Arabs out and to keep the Jews in."(47)

During his January 23, 1945 conversation with the President, Dr. Wise proposed that the "immediate need of the hour was large immigration, and ships, goods, medicine, etc. What was needed was mass transportation of Jews to Palestine." The President responded by saying that the Arabs were "afraid of the Jews" and he referred to the Jews as infiltrating into Trans-Jordan. Dr. Wise tried to reassure him that the Jews were not interested in Trans-Jordan and concluded that "We stand behind you Mr. President. We expect you to support us. You have expressed your sympathy with us and we believe you mean it. All Zionists are with you." President Roosevelt puffed on his cigarette and asked smilingly: "Did you say all?" "Would you be willing to put a fence around Palestine?" "Yes," answered the rabbi, "you keep the Arabs out and we will keep the Jews in."(48)

So it was on January 23. Wise and Roosevelt would again meet on March 16, at which time the President would again reassure him of his good will.

But on February 14, 1945, Roosevelt met with King Saud, and he asked him for advice regarding the Jews. Saud said that the Jews should be granted "living space" in the Axis countries which had oppressed them. Roosevelt concurred, "the Germans appear to have killed three million Polish Jews, by which count there should be space in Poland for the resettlement of many homeless Jews."(49)

Roosevelt reassured the Arab king that "he would do nothing to assist the Jews against the Arabs and would make no move hostile to the Arab people," and when Saud proposed to send an Arab mission to America to present the case of the Arabs and Palestine, F.D.R. said it would be "a very good idea because he thought many people in America and England are misinformed."(50)

In early March, Colonel Hoskins met with F.D.R. and the First Lady. Among other things they discussed were Erez Israel and the Jews. According to Hoskins' notes of the meeting, F.D.R. was very pessimistic about Jewish chances in Palestine, but Mrs. Roosevelt was very pro-Zionist. She spoke of the "wonderful work that had been done by the Zionists in certain parts of Palestine." The President noted that on his flight over Palestine he found the area to be "extremely rocky and barren" except along the coastal plain. When Mrs. Roosevelt noted that the Zionists now felt much stronger and were ready to risk a fight for their homeland, the President reminded her that there were some 20 million Arabs in and around Palestine and he thought that "in the long run these numbers would win out."(51)

But in his March 16 conversations with Wise, the President said that he was still in favor of unrestricted Jewish immigration and a Jewish State in Palestine. Wise reported that the "most important thing of all," was that F.D.R. was "resolved to help us." While the President knew of Saud's limitations, "somebody in the State Department or in London" had given him the impression that Saud was an "important figure" and he had "overestimated" him. "I'm sorry to say I utterly failed with regard to Ibn Saud," said Roosevelt. Wise believed that Roosevelt was "absolutely resolved to appeal from an Ibn Saud drunk to a greater Ibn Saud sober - to some court of high appeal, to bring our case there."(52)

At conversation's end, Rabbi Wise asked the President if he would sign a statement on Palestine. "Certainly I will sign it," said Roosevelt.(53) Thus the March 16 statement pointing to the President's support was issued. That statement, intended as it was to assuage Zionist apprehension concerning Roosevelt's intentions, almost brought the State Department house down. Wallace Murray warned that the President's statement would have "serious repercussions in the Near East" and "a most far-reaching effect upon American interest throughout the area."(54)

On April 5, President Roosevelt reassured Saud that "no decision would be taken without full consultation with both Arabs and Jews." Roosevelt promised once again that he "would take no action, in my capacity as Chief of the Executive Branch of this Government, which might prove hostile to the Arab people."(55)

Thus the diplomacy of Roosevelt. It was two-faced, tricky and disasterous for the Jews. It was part of the game of international politics which the leaders of the world played, with little, if any, regard for the people involved. Some may call it diplomacy, others may call it sinisterism. Whatever you may wish to call it is up to you. Roosevelt and the British acted in such a manner as to prevent the rescue of European Jewry. Their policies enabled the Nazi Germans and their European collaborators to slaughter six million Jewish men, women and children.

1 Robert Szold Papers
2 *Ibid.*
3 Memo of telephone conversation between David Ben Gurion and Rabbi Stephen S. Wise, May 12, 1937, Wise Papers, Brandeis University; *Foreign Relations of the United States*, July 7, 1937, II, 889-890.
4 *Foreign Relations of the United States*, November 10; December 2, 1937, II 921-922.
5 *Foreign Relations of the United States*, September 17, 1937, II, 909-922.

6  Morris D. Waldman to Wallace Murray, Letter, September 25, 1943, State Department File No. 867N.01/1993, National Archives, Washington D.C. In his autobiography *Nor by Power* (New York, 1953) Waldman made no mention of his anti-Zionist intervention with Wallace Murray.
7  Memo from Division of Near Eastern Affairs on Conversation between Wallace Murray and Morris D. Waldman, September 29, 1943, State Department File No. 967N.01/1999½, National Archives, Washington, D.C.
8  *Ibid.*
9  Near East Division Memo, January 10, 1944, B. Long Papers, The Library of Congress.
10  *Ibid.*
11  Summary of American Jewish Committee Position, November 8, 1943, Palestine Files, American Jewish Committee Archives, New York.
12  Richard E. Gutstadt to Justice Brandeis, August 16, 1940, Robert Szold Papers.
13  S.S. Wise Memo on conversations with F.D.R., January 22, 1938, S.S. Wise Papers, Brandeis University.
14  Louis D. Brandeis to Stephen S. Wise, November 16, 1938; Stephen S. Wise to Robert Szold, December 27, 1938, Robert Szold Papers.
15  Chaim Weizmann to Nahum Goldmann, Louis Lipsky, Stephen S. Wise, October 6, 1938; F.D.R. to William Green, May 3, 1939, Robert Szold Papers. While he himself was not a Zionist, Bernard Baruch supported the proposition that the Jews should be given the opportunity to settle in Palestine and he presented Roosevelt with a water irrigation plan according to which a series of wells would be dug above the Jordan and the water would be used to irrigate the surrounding area for the settlement of some 120,000 Jews. The Arabs of the area had approved the project for which Baruch could raise $150,000. Nothing came of the project. See memo signed by Aranow, Nov. 1, 1938, Robert Szold Papers.
16  *Foreign Relations of the United States,* March 10, 1939, IV, 731.
17  Chaim Weizmann to Justice Brandeis, April 19, 1939, Robert Szold Papers.
18  Britain did not permit even the 100,000 to enter Erez Israel.
19  *Foreign Relations of the United States,* May 17, 1939, IV, 757.
20  Stephen S. Wise Memorandum dated May 22, 1939, Robert Szold Papers.
21  *Ibid.*
22  *Foreign Relations of the United States,* July 21, 1939, II, 791-793.
23  David Ben Gurion to Justice Brandeis, June 6, 1939, Robert Szold Papers.

## 100  To the Promised Land

24  David Ben Gurion Memo, November 14, 1940, Robert Szold Papers.

25  American Emergency Committee for Zionist Affairs. Zionist Public Relations Committee Throughout America. *Manual for their Organization and Function* (New York, 1943), 7-8, Zionist Archives, New York.

26  F.D.R. to Stephen S. Wise, June 9, 1941, Robert Szold Papers.

27  *Ibid.*

28  Special British advisor to Ibn Saud.

29  *Foreign Relations of the United States,* June 12, 1943, 795.

30  *Ibid.*

31  *Ibid.* August 31, 1943, IV, 807-810.

32  *Ibid.*, September 27, 1943, IV, 811-814.

33  Chaim Weizmann, *Trial and Error* (New York, 1949), 427-433.

34  *Ibid.*

35  Nahum Goldmann to Stephen S. Wise, January 17, 1944, Robert Szold Papers.

36  *Ibid., Foreign Relations of the United States,* February 3, 1944, V, 562-563.

37  *Ibid.*

38  Ben Gurion meeting U.S. Zionist leaders Louis Lipsky, Robert Szold, Nahum Goldmann, S.S. Wise, December 5, 1940, Individuals Files, Zionist Archives, New York.

39  Minutes of meeting with Chaim Weizmann, Jule 17, 1941, B. Akzin Folders of American Zionist Emergency Council Papers, Zionist Archives, New York.

40  *Ibid.*

41 *Ibid.*

42  *Foreign Relations of the United States,* February 3, 1944, V, 562-563.

43  *Foreign Relations of the United States*, February 22, 1944, V, 574-576.

44  B. Long Memorandum, February 24, 1944, B. Long Papers, Library of Congress.

45  Robert Szold Papers.

46  *New York Times,* March 17, 1944.

47  Stephen S. Wise to Felix Frankfurter, January 28, 1945, Stephen S. Wise Papers, Brandeis University.

48  Stephen S. Wise Conference with F.D.R., January 23, 1945, President's File, 1943-1945, American Zionist Emergency Council Papers, Zionist Archives, New York.

49  *Foreign Relations of the United States,* February 14, 1945, VIII, 1-2; William A. Eddy, *F.D.R. Meets Ibn Saud* (New York, 1954) 311-316.

50  *Ibid.*, Hoskins to Alling, March 5, 1945, VIII, 690-691.
51  *Ibid.*
52  Wise Memo on Conference held with F.D.R., March 16, 1945, President's Files, 1943-1945, American Zionist Emergency Committee Papers, Zionist Archives, New York.
53  *Ibid.*
54  *Foreign Relations of the United States*, March 20, 1945, VIII, 694-695.
55  *Ibid.*, F.D.R. to King of Saudi Arabia, April 5, 1945, 698.

# BIBLIOGRAPHY

*Bibliographical Sources:*
The following books refer to *some* of the published materials available on the period of the Holocaust. It is included in this work in the hope that the reader may wish to further investigate and research this subject.

*General Works:*
Able, T. *The Nazi Movement: Why Hitler Came to Power* (New York, 1966).
Adorno, T.W., *The Authoritarian Personality* (New York, 1950).
Alport, G. *The Nature of Prejudice* (New York, 1958).
Bides, M.D. *Father of Racist Ideology: The Social and Political Thought of Count Gobineau* (New York, 1970).
Bracker, K.D., *The German Dictatorship. The Origins, Structure and Effects of National Socialism* (New York, 1970).
Cecil, R.*The Myth of the Master Race: Alfred Rosenberg and Nazi Ideology* (London, 1972).
Clark, C., *Eichmann: The Man and His Crimes* (New York, 1960).
Cohn, N. *Warrant for Genocide: A History of the Protocals of the Elders of Zion* (New York, 1967).
Colodner, S., *Jewish Education in Germany Under the Nazis* (New York, 1964).
Davidson, E., *The Trial of the Germans* (New York, 1966).
Dimont, M., *The Indestructable Jews* (New York, 1973).
Druks, H., *From Truman through Johnson*, Volume I (New York, 1971).
Gilbert, G.M., *Nuremberg Diary* (New York, 1961).
Glatstein, Jacob, *Anthology of Holocaust Literature,* (Philadelphia, 1970).
Glianda, Jurgis, *House Upon the Sand* (Maryland, 1963).
Grunberger, R., *The 12 year Reich* (New York, 1972).

Handlin, O., *A Continuing Task, The J.D.C.* (New York, 1969).
Harris, W.R., *Tyranny on Trial, The Evidence at Nuremberg* (Texas, 1954).
Hausner, G. *Justice in Jerusalem: The Eichmann Trial* (New York, 1966).
Hill M., and N.L. Williams, *Auschwitz in England, A Record of a Libel Action* (London, 1965).
Kohn, H. *The Mind of Germany* (New York, 1960).

Lewy, G., *The Catholic Church and Nazi Germany* (New York, 1964).
Littlejohn, D., *The Patriotic Traitors, The History of Collaboration in German-Occupied Europe 1940-1945* (New York, 1972).
Manchester, William, *The Arms of Krupp* (Boston, 1968).
Massing, P.W. *Rehearsal for Destruction, A Study of Political Anti-Semitism in Imperial Germany* (New York, 1949).
Poliakov, L. *Harvest of Hate* (Syracuse, 1954).
Robinson, J. and Philip Friedman, *Guide to Jewish History Under Nazi Impact (New York, 1960).*
Russell, Lord of Liverpool, *The Record, The Trial of Eichmann* (New York, 1963).
Simth, B.F., *Adolf Hitler: His Family, Childhood, and Youth* (Stanford, 1967).
Snell, J.L. ed., *The Nazi Revolution* (Boston, 1959).
Snell, J.L., *The Outbreak of the Second World War* (Boston, 1962).
Snyder, L.L., *The War* (New York, 1960).
Snyder, L.L., *Hitler and Nazism* (New York, 1961).

Speer, A. *Inside the Third Reich* (New York, 1970).
Taylor, A.J.P. *The Origins of the Second World War* (New York, 1966).
Waite, R.G.L., *The Psychopathic God Adolf Hitler* (New York, 1977).
Yad Vashem Publications, Jerusalem: *Bulletins, Studies, News, Blackbooks of Localities.*
Zahn, G. *German Catholics and Hitler's Wars* (New York, 1962).


*State Policies, Ghettos and Camps:*
Borzykowski, Tuvia, *Between Tumbling Walls* (Beit Lohamei Hagettaot, Israel).
Braham, R. *Eichmann and the Destruction of Hungarian Jewry* (New York, 1961).
Chary, F.B. *The Bulgarian Jews and the Final Solution* (Pittsburg, 1972).
Cohen, E.A., *Human Behavior in the Concentration Camps* (New York, 1953).
Delarue, J., *The Gestapo: A History of Horror* (New York, 1964).
Donat, A., *The Holocaust Kingdom* (New York, 1965).
Flender, H., *Rescue in Denmark* (New York, 1963).
Frankel, V.E., *Man's Search For Meaning* (Boston, 1963).
Friedlander, Saul, *Pius XII and the Third Reich* (New York, 1966).
Garfinkel, L. *The Destruction of Jewish Kovno* (Jerusalem, 1959).
Goldstein, B. *The Stars Bear Witness* (New York, 1949).
Hashomer Hatzair *The Massacre of European Jewry, An Anthology* (Israel, 1963).
Jasny, W., *The Extermination of Lodz Jews* (Tel Aviv, 1950).

Kaplan, C.A., *Scroll of Agony* (New York, 1965).
Katz, R. *Death in Rome* (New York, 1968).
Kogon, E., *The Theory and Practice of Hell: The Concentration Camp and the System Behind Them* (New York, 1950).
Kraus, C., *The Death Factory: Documents on Auschwitz* (Oxford, 1966).
Lazar, A.O., *Innocents Condemned to Death* (New York, 1961).
Meed, V., *On Both Sides of the Wall* (Israel, 1972).
Misterlich, A. *Doctors of Infamy* (New York, 1949).
Muszkat, M., *Polish Charges Against German War Criminals*, (Warsaw, 1948).
Poliakov, L. and J. Sabille, *Jews Under the Italian Occupation* (Paris, 1955).
Presser, J., *The Destruction of the Dutch Jews* (New York, 1969).
Ringelblum, E. *Notes from the Warsaw Ghetto* (New York, 1958).
Steiner, J. *Treblinka* (New York, 1967).
Trunk, I., *Judenrat* (New York, 1973).
Yahil, L., *The Rescue of Danish Jewry* (Philadelphia, 1969).
World Jewish Congress, *Extermination of Polish Jewry: Reports Based on Official Documents* (New York, 1947).
World Jewish Congress and American Jewish Congress, *Hitler's Ten Year War On The Jews* (New York, 1943).

*Resistance:*
Barkai, M., *The Fighting Ghettos* (Philadelphia, 1962).
Bartoscewski, W., *The Samaritans, Heroes of the Holocaust* (New York, 1970).
Bar-Zohar, M. *The Avengers* (New York, 1970).
Bauer, Y. *They Chose Life* (New York, 1973).
Boehm, E.H. *We Survived* (New Haven, 1949).
Congress for Jewish Culture, *The Warsaw Ghetto Uprising* (New York, 1972).
Cowarn, L., *Children of the Resistance* (New York, 1969).
Donat, A. *Jewish Resistance* (New York, 1965).
Edelman, M., *The Ghetto Fights* (New York, 1946).
Friedman, P., *Martyrs and Fighters: Epic of the Warsaw Ghetto* (New York, 1954).
Friedman, P., *Their Brothers Keeper: The Christian Heroes and Heroines Who Helped The Oppressed Escape the Nazi Terror* (New York, 1957).
Friedman, Tuvia, *The Hunter* (New York, 1961).
Kibbutz Lahamei Haghettaot, *Extermination and Resistance: Historical Record and Source Material* (Israel, 1958).
Latour, A., *La Resistance Juive en France* (Paris, 1970).

Meed, V., *On Both Sides of the Wall* (Israel, 1972).
Mirenstein, A., *A Tower From The Enemy: Contributions to History of Jewish Resistance in Poland* (New York, 1959).
Muskat, M., *Jewish Soldiers in the War Against the Nazis* (Jerusalem, 1972).
Ravine, J., *La Resistance Organisee des Juifs en France* (Paris, 1973).
Shabbetai, K., *As Sheep to the Slaughter: The Myth of Cowardice* (New York, 1963).
Shul, Y., *They Fought Back* (New York, 1967).
Sternberg, L., *The Revolt of the Jews* (Paris, 1970).
Tenenbaum, J., *Underground* (New York, 1952).
Tenenbaum, J. *We Have Not Forgotten* (Warsaw, 1961).
Tushnet, L. *To Die with Honor: The Uprising of the Jews of the Warsaw Ghetto* (New York, 1965).
Winocour, J. *The Jewish Resistance* (New York, 1968).
Yad Vashem, *Jewish Resistance During the Holocaust Period* (Jerusalem, 1971).
Yanai, N. and M. Tzur, *The Holocaust* (American Zionist Youth Foundation, New York, 1970).

*Rescue:*
Bauer, Y. *Bricha, The Organized Escape of the Jewish Survivors of Eastern Europe, 1944-1948* (New York, 1970).
Bentwich, N., *They Found Refuge* (London, 1956)
Feingold, H., *Politics of Rescue* (Rutgers Univ., 1970).
Flender, H., *Rescue in Denmark* (New York, 1963).
Friedman, S., *No Haven for the Oppressed* (Wayne Univ., 1973).
Friedman, T., *The Hunter* (New York, 1961).
Kluger, R., and P. Mann, *The Last Escape* (New York, 1973).
MacDonald, J.G., *My Mission to Israel* (New York, 1951).
Morse, A. *While Six Million Died* (New York, 1969).
Weisberg, A., *Desperate Mission, Joel Brand's Story* (New York, 1958).
World Jewish Congress, *Unity in Dispersion* (New York, 1948).


*Diaries, Memoirs:*
Adler, H.G., *Theresienstadt 1941-1945* (Tubingen, 1955).
Boehm, E.H., *We Survived* (Yale, 1949).
Boyle, K. *Breaking the Silence* (Institute of Human Relations, 1962).
Chabban, B., *Rescued Children* (Tel Aviv, 1946).
Cospary, Vera, *A Chosen Sparrow* (New York, 1964).
David, J., *A Touch of Earth - A Wartime Childhood* (New York, 1969).
Donat, A. *Holocaust Kingdom* (New York, 1965).

Frank, A., *The Diary of a Young Girl* (New York, 1967).
Gershon, K., *We Came as Children* (London, 1966).
Goldstein, B. *The Stars Bear Witness* (New York, 1949).
Kaplan, C.A. *Scroll of Agony* (New York, 1965).
Kardoff, U. *Diary of Nightmare* (New York, 1966).
Kuchler-Silverman, L. *One Hundred Children* (New York, 1967).
Neshamit, S., *The Children of Mapu Street* (Philadelphia, 1970).
Ringelblum, E. *Notes from the Warsaw Ghetto* (New York, 1958).
Rosen, D., *The Forest, My Friend* (New York, 1971).
Sachs, Nelly *O The Chimneys* (New York, 1967).
Senesh, H., *The Diary, Letters, Poems and Mission of Hanna Senesh* (London, 1971).
Wells, L. *The Jankowska Road* (New York, 1963).

*Literature:*
Forsyth, F., *The Odessa File* (New York, 1972).
Grossman, L., *The Shop on Main Street* (New York, 1970).
Habe, Hans, *The Mission* (New York, 1966).
Hersey, J. *The Wall (New York, 1951)*.

Kuznetsov, A., *Babi Yar: A Documentary Novel* (New York, 1971).
Schwartz-Bart, Andre, *The Last of the Just* (New York, 1961).
Uris, L., *Mila 18* (New York, 1961).

*War Trials:*
Davidson, E., *The Trial of the Germans* (New York, 1966).
Hausner, G., *Justice in Jerusalem* (New York, 1968).
Klarsfeld, Beate, *Wherever They May Be!* (New York, 1975).

# INDEX

Adler, Cyrus,   2, 7.
Alexander, Robert,   46, 52.
Alien Registration Act   10.
Aliyah Bet   91.

Backe, Herman   35.
Balfour, Arthur,   83.
Baruch, Bernard,   3, 9, 77.
Belzec   31.
Ben Gurion, David,   91.
Berenson, Lawrence,   19, 21-22.
Bermuda Conference   39-44, 45, 47, 77.
Berry, Burton Y.,   61.
Biltmore Conference   95.
Bloom, Sol,   39, 45, 47.
Brand, Joel,   58-63.
Bromfield, Louis,   77.
Bru, Laredo,   17, 18, 19, 21, 24.

Cavert, Samuel,   3.
Celler, Emanuel,   46.

Chamberlain, Neville,   4, 8, 9.
Churchill, Winston,   4, 36, 43, 93.
Crystal Night   5, 6.

Dodd, William E.,   11.
Dunn, Clement,   38.

Eden, Anthony,   4, 42, 70, 72.
Eichmann, Adolf,   58-60, 64.
Evian,   3-5, 7, 77.
Europa Plan   58, 59.

Fleischmann, Gisi,   58.

Goldmann, Nahum,   7, 9, 25, 31, 37, 67, 68, 93.
Green, William,   12.

Harriman, Averell W.,   52.
Harrison, Leland,   33, 37, 38.
Hecht, Ben, 36, 77.
Himmler, Heinrich,   58, 73-75.
Hirschmann, Ira,   46, 61, 71.
Hitler, Adolf,   4, 34, 35, 45, 51, 65, 74.
Hoskins, Halford,   93-97.
Hull, Cordell,   6, 44, 50, 52, 53, 91.

Ittleson, Henry,   20.

Jabotinsky, Vladimir,   91.
Jenkins, Newton,   6.
Jewish Agency   39.
Jewish Telegraphic Agency   36.
Joint Distribution Committee   17-26, 30, 58, 69.

Kaufman, Ed,   23.
Kennedy, Joseph P.,   7, 8.
Kennedy, Louis,   3, 24.
Kubowitzki, Leon,   65-69.

Leahy, William D.,   42.
Lipsky, Louis,   7, 9.
Lindsay, Ronald,   8.
Law, Richard,   66.
Lodge, Henry Cabot,   84.
Long, Breckinridge,   10, 42, 45, 95.

## Index

McCloy, John J., 65, 67, 68.
Mazur, Norbert, 73-75.
Marcantonio, Vito, 77.
Messersmith, George, 6.
Mikoljczyk, Stanslaw, 64.
Morgenthau, Henry, Jr., 3, 44, 47, 77.
Morse, Arthur, 46.
Moyne, Lord, 61.
Murray, Wallace, 85, 86.
Mussolini, Benito, 4, 10.

Neumann, Emanuel, 2, 4.
Niles, David K., 93.

O'Dwyer, William, 81.
*Orduna* 22.
Oscwiecim, 31.
Oswego, 1, 79-83.

Pehle, John, 65.
Perlzweig, Maurice L., 33.
Pius XII 47, 48, 49.

*Quanza* 10.

Reynolds, Robert R., 81.
Rogers, Will Jr., 77.
Roncalli, Angelo, 51.
Rosenberg, James N., 19, 23, 88.
Rosenman, Samuel I., 6.
Rothschild, Lord, 5.
Riegner, Gerhard, 31-33, 75.

Sagalowitz, Benjamin, 32.
Saud, Ibn, 93, 96, 97, 98.
Schwartzbart, Ignacy, 64.
Sharett, Moshe, 60-61, 66.
Silver, Abba Hillel, 95, 96.
Silverman, Sidney, 33, 34.
Smuts, Jan C., 53.
Sobibor, 31.
Stalin, Josef, 36.
Steinhardt, Lawrence, 11-12, 69, 88.
Stettinius, Edward, 44, 47.
Stimson, Henry L. 47, 51, 95.
*St. Louis,* 17-26.
Szold, Henrietta, 96.
Szold, Robert, 9.

Treblinka, 31.

Waldman, Morris D., 86, 88.
War Refugee Board 26, 47-53, 57, 62, 63, 74.
Warburg, Felix, 85.
Warren, Avra M., 22, 46.
Weizmann, Chaim, 39-41, 53, 64, 66, 88, 92.
Welles, Sumner, 19, 32, 38, 43.
Wilson, Woodrow, 83, 84.
Wise, Stephen S. 2, 3, 5, 12, 30, 31, 37, 81, 85, 97, 98.
Wisliceny, Dieter, 58.
World Jewish Congress 31-36,

Vaad Hahatzala, 69.
Virgin Islands, 9.